He

The silence began to quiver with an awkward tension. His dark eyes probed hers and she felt her stomach flutter uneasily. Why was he looking at her like that? What was it that he was thinking and not saying? She tried to say something to break the silence, some clever remark that would make him smile, but no thoughts nor words presented themselves.

She couldn't move, couldn't tear her eyes away.

"It's just as well you're not Cinderella," he said softly. He paused for a fraction of a moment, his eyes still holding hers captive. "I'm no prince, Samantha."

KAREN VAN DER ZEE grew up in Holland and as a child wanted to do two things: write books and travel. She's been very lucky. Her American husband's work as a development economist has taken them to many exotic locations. They were married in Kenya, had their first daughter in Ghana and their second in the United States. The family, which now includes a son, currently lives in Virginia.

KAREN VAN DER ZEE

Something in Return

Harlequin Books

TORONTO • NEW YORK • LONDON
AMSTERDAM • PARIS • SYDNEY • HAMBURG
STOCKHOLM • ATHENS • TOKYO • MILAN
MADRID • WARSAW • BUDAPEST • AUCKLAND

ISBN 0-373-11630-6

SOMETHING IN RETURN

CHAPTER ONE

If thou must love me, let it be for naught
Except for love's sake only.

Elizabeth Barrett Browning:
Sonnets from the Portuguese XIV

"SAM, there's a *limo* outside! A *stretch limo* with a *driver* inside!"

Samantha stepped over a box of canned soup and searched the room for David's skinny frame and bald head. The school cafeteria this Friday night was crowded with ACTION volunteers, boxes of food, tables of food, bags of food, all donated by area citizens for their needy neighbours.

"Sam! Didn't you hear what I said? There's a *giant limousine* sitting outside!"

Samantha looked at Melissa's excited face and frowned. "Yeah, I heard you." She tucked a dark curl back over her ear. "I don't know anything about it. I suppose it belongs to the guy over there." She waved her hand across the room at the tall dark man in the three-piece business suit. She'd been aware of him for the last ten minutes or so, wondering what he was doing here, but she'd been too busy to find out.

Melissa looked. "Oh, wow," she whispered. "Where did he come from?"

"I don't know. I don't *care* right now. I need David. Did you see him anywhere?"

"No. Why?"

"He has the list. Social Services called me with another name—a woman with two kids. Her husband took off with their only car, their checkbook, all their savings,

5

the dog and the TV. Oh, there he is!'' Samantha dashed off across the room.

"David!" She grabbed his thin arm. "I have one more name. Here." She gave him a slip of paper.

He took it from her. "Thanks." He gestured across the room. "Who's that character over there?"

She glanced at the tall, imposing man standing by the door, surveying the goings-on with sharp, dark eyes. He looked totally out of place in his three-piece suit, white shirt and tie. Behind him a dark overcoat lay draped over a chair. There was no doubt in her mind that the limousine Melissa had mentioned belonged to him, or at least that he'd arrived in it.

"I have no idea," she said. She'd never seen the man before and he certainly didn't look like a volunteer who'd come to help out. What he did look like was totally and completely immaculate. Someone from another world. A very rich world where nobody was in need of canned pea soup.

She wiped some flour off the front of her red sweatshirt. She was wearing sweatpants to match, and old, comfortable running shoes. Her long hair was escaping from the rubber band and she took it out, shook it and tied it back again. When it came to immaculate, she wasn't going to win any prizes, but when it came to looking cheerful she was doing a lot better than the man by the door.

She didn't know much about men's clothing—brand names, styles, or fabrics—but even from a distance it was easy to see that his suit had not been bought off the rack at a department store. Everything about him was crisp, clean and elegant. He radiated authority and quiet composure, and it was difficult not to be affected by all this male splendor.

What was he doing here?

Well, there was one way to find out. She poured herself a cup of coffee, lacing it liberally with both sugar and cream, and sauntered over to the stranger.

"Hi," she said, extending her right hand. "I'm Samantha Greene. I saw you standing here and wondered if there's anything I can do for you."

He took her hand, deep brown eyes meeting hers. "Ramsey MacMillan. I believe I'm meant to observe the proceedings." His voice was deep and calm. He had a Roman nose, she saw, and a square, prominent chin. His features were angular and well defined. It was an arresting face, rather than handsome. A very masculine face.

"I'm not sure I understand," she said.

He gave her a level look. "I'm not sure I do, either."

She smiled. "Ah, I love a mystery. I take it the limo outside is yours?"

"It is."

"How did you end up here? I mean, who told you to come here?"

"My cousin Alicia." He gave a short nod indicating the place where Alicia, in designer jeans and sweater, was sorting through grocery bags full of donated food. "She dragged me here from Washington under false pretenses."

"False pretenses? Sounds exciting." Alicia was the representative of an area church. She was beautiful, rich, and well connected. Also sincere, enthusiastic and very creative in finding solutions. "What did she tell you?" asked Samantha.

"She said she was taking me out to dinner to discuss a serious financial matter."

"She did, did she?" Samantha bit her lip trying to control the laughter bubbling up inside her. Alicia had a bizarre sense of humor. "I see. Well, dinner's over there." She pointed at the table near the kitchen where an assortment of hot casseroles, salads and rolls was laid out for the volunteers. "It's great stuff. Try it." She surveyed his immaculate suit. He probably had not been expecting to eat tuna-noodle casserole in the cafeteria room of a rather seedy-looking elementary school in the boonies of Virginia. She hadn't had time to eat yet herself; it would have to wait until things were in progress.

The man made no move toward the food. "What's going on here?" he asked, glancing around imperiously.

Obviously a man who was used to being in command, who demanded to be in the know, Samantha decided. "We're making up boxes of food for Thanksgiving for needy families," she said obligingly. "The community has been collecting food for the past few weeks—the schools, churches, the Boy Scouts, the Rotary Clubs, everybody. We do the same for Christmas."

"I see." He glanced back at her. "How many needy families are we talking about?"

"Ninety-three."

His face showed no reaction. He had a tan, she noticed, and that in November. Not all his time lately had been spent in the Washington, D.C., area, that was clear.

The food had all been sorted and volunteers began to line up to take their numbered boxes to fill them for the individual families.

"So why *did* Alicia bring you here?" she asked when he remained quiet.

"She wants my money, no doubt."

Samantha nodded. "We can use it."

"So can everybody else."

"Of course." She felt the little devil inside her begin to act up. "Excuse me for a moment." She walked up to David, who was handing out the boxes.

"Give me one," she said.

"Here. One adult, three children."

She took the box back to Ramsey MacMillan and thrust it into his hands. "Here, get this filled up. One adult, three children."

He looked down at the box in his hands as if he wasn't sure he was going to hold on to it. One dark brow quirked. "What's that supposed to mean?"

"You get in line with the rest of the people. At every table you tell them you need stuff for one adult and three children and they'll give you whatever they're handing out—vegetables or flour or spaghetti. It's real easy," she said reassuringly. "You don't even have to think."

"Well, that's a relief."

She grinned. The sight of him appealed to her sense of the absurd. He looked utterly out of place in his expensive suit, clutching the cardboard box to his chest. Everybody else was in jeans and sweaters, and here he stood, arrogant and regal, looking as if he belonged at a high-powered board meeting.

"I'll take your coat," she said helpfully. "I'll put it in the kitchen."

He didn't move, his eyes locking with hers. She held his gaze, trying not to laugh, determined not to break it. Nothing was going to make her lower her eyes. Then he put the box on the floor and shouldered out of his suit jacket, all the while looking right into her eyes. He handed her the jacket. "Take this too, please," he said calmly. He took out the gold cuff links, slipped them into his pocket and rolled up his shirtsleeves, revealing tanned, muscled arms lightly dusted with dark hair. He wore an expensive-looking watch, but, not being an expert on things fancy, she could not identify its lofty origins. He picked up the box from the floor.

With his coat and jacket clutched to her chest, Samantha watched him move into line. He was actually doing it! She couldn't believe it. Another laugh escaped her, and a delicious sense of mischief filled her. She put his things in the kitchen and went back into the cafeteria.

"Sam!" Alicia came up to her, smoothing down her gleaming cap of auburn hair. She was in her early thirties, but looked much younger. Her face was made up to perfection, and diamond earrings sparkled in the light. "Where is he?"

Samantha pointed. "Over there, with the baked beans."

Alicia gaped, then she laughed. "This is hilarious! How did you get him to do that?"

"I gave him a box and told him to go stand in line."

"Ramsey MacMillan doesn't stand in lines."

"He does now."

Alicia swallowed her laughter. "What did you say to him? You must have *said* something!"

"Nothing. Just to go fill up the box."

"And he just did it?" Alicia's tone ran over with disbelief.

"Yeah." Samantha grinned.

"You must have magic powers. Oh, Lord, I wish I had my camera! Wait till my husband hears this—he's not going to believe it. Ramsey's such a stuck-up son of a bitch."

"He's your cousin?"

"Yes. We were close as kids, although I'm from the poor branch of the family." Alicia grinned. "Relatively speaking."

Samantha hoped so. The word poor did not occur to you in connection with Alicia, whose prestigious address, expensive clothes and snappy silver Saab rather oozed financial well-being.

They were interrupted by David, who needed assistance, and work claimed Samantha's attention. Yet every now and then she couldn't help searching the room for Ramsey. Some strange force seemed to pull her gaze toward him, wanting to look at his tall, straight figure in shirtsleeves. There was something very compelling about this man, about his dark eyes, his composed manner.

He appeared at her side about an hour later. "Done," he said with finality, pushing his hands into his pant pockets. "I did three rounds. Satisfied?"

She met his dark eyes. "We appreciate your help," she said with a polite smile. As she spoke the words, her stomach growled inelegantly. "I believe I'd better have something to eat now. Would you care to join me?"

"Why not?" He moved with her to the table with the cooked food. They helped themselves and found a couple of chairs to sit on.

"Why did Alicia bring you here?" Samantha asked after the first few bites had appeased her stomach. "Why didn't she just ask for your money?"

"She wanted me to see this so it would melt my heart and I'd be willing to part with more of the green stuff."

She nodded. "Money is nice."

"You think so?"

"Oh, yes. You can do lots of wonderful things with money." She gave him a bright smile.

"What kind of wonderful things?"

"Well, it depends on how much money we're talking about, of course. But say we have a pile of it. We'd—"

"Say *you* have a pile of it."

She gave a surprised little laugh. "Me? Personally?"

"Right. You, personally. What do you need?"

The question took her by surprise. "Oh, I don't need anything."

"Everybody needs something."

"I've got everything I need. I have a great job, a roof over my head, a wood stove and a car that gets me where I want to go."

"All right, if you don't *need* anything, what do you *want*? For yourself."

She stared at him. What did she want? She began to laugh. "I don't know. Honestly, I'm happy."

The dark eyes surveyed her calmly. There was something about those eyes that almost made her nervous, as if they tried to see straight into her head. As if, if she ever told a lie, he'd know it.

"There must be something you want. I've never heard of anybody who didn't want anything."

He was right, of course. There was something she wanted, but it wasn't something she was going to divulge to a total stranger.

"What about jewelry, plastic surgery?"

She nearly choked on a green bean. "Plastic surgery?" She laughed—she couldn't help it. "Are you a surgeon pushing your services?"

His mouth twitched. "No. I thought all women wanted plastic surgery these days, whether they needed it or not."

"Well, not me. I like myself just fine." Not that she was gorgeous, but everything more or less sat where it belonged and more or less had the right shape and size. Okay, okay, she said to herself. You look good, you know you do. Maybe not in this outfit, but with a little effort you're quite presentable.

He gave her a searching look. "Very commendable. What about jewelry, clothes, travel? You must want something."

She shrugged. "I make most of my own clothes. The things in the stores are either boring or too expensive. I don't care much for fancy jewelry. I like earrings, but I'm not really interested in the expensive stuff." She frowned, thinking. "Travel." Visions sprang up in her imagination and she gave a triumphant laugh. "I know what I want! I almost forgot. Some day I'd love to go on safari to Kenya and Tanzania, see the animals. Especially the elephants, if they aren't extinct by then. I love elephants."

"You love elephants."

"Yes. But I feel sorry for them in the zoo. I'd just love to see them in the wild. I keep thinking, it must be like the Garden of Eden, to see all these beautiful creatures roaming free in their natural state. There's something terribly wrong with the world, you know, that we don't take care of the earth. We're destroying the rain forests and the animals, and people are starving...oh, here I go again. Sorry, sorry. Anyway, look at this." She gestured around the room. "This is wonderful. We're doing something here." She took another forkful of food. "Maybe in the big picture it isn't much, but it means something to the people we help."

"Everyone here is a volunteer?" he queried.

"Right. ACTION has no paid employees."

"What's that great job you were talking about?"

"Oh, that's not with ACTION. I'm a teacher. First grade, right here." She waved her fork around indicating the school building. "My classroom is right across the hall, the one with the three-eyed clown on the door."

It would most likely be her last year here. The school building was old and new schools were being built in nearby suburbs. Seeing Aurora Elementary go would be hard, and it wasn't something she allowed herself to think about often.

Alicia approached the table and sat down with them. The diamond earrings were shooting sparks around the room. She smiled at Ramsey, who gave her a long, dark stare.

"What happened to the dress?" he asked.

Alicia gave a casual shrug. "I changed in the ladies' room." She bit her lip. "I'm sorry I played this trick on you, but I had to find a way to get you out here."

"And you let me think that you, my beloved cousin, were in dire financial straits, and I had to come to the rescue." Ramsey paused meaningfully. "I had to postpone a business dinner for this."

Alicia bit her glossy lip and looked repentant. "I'll never forgive myself. I hope you'll still feel moved to make a lavish donation to ACTION."

"We'll see." He brought another forkful of food to his mouth, then thought better of it and lowered it back to his plate.

"You can see we're trying to help," Alicia went on. "Look at all the volunteers. Isn't it great?"

"Delightful," he said dryly. "As is the food."

"What's wrong with it?" Samantha asked.

"Nothing, absolutely nothing, if you like lukewarm overcooked soggy tuna-noodle casserole."

Samantha had to admit he had a point. The food had been sitting around too long to be appetizing anymore.

"You're a brave soldier," Alicia said brightly, biting into a piece of chocolate cake. Samantha wondered if Alicia was going to get away unpunished with the trick she had played on Ramsey MacMillan. It must have taken quite a bit of courage; he didn't seem a man you'd want to fool around with. Yet there were no outward

signs of wrath. He was controlled and composed. Maybe
having money and wearing expensive clothes did that to
you. She examined the tie above the waistcoat. Dark,
with tiny white pin dots. Hyper-conservative, no imagination, she concluded. Why not something brighter,
more colourful?

"Did I spill something?" he asked, dark brows raised.

"Oh, no." She bit her lip, the devil doing a dance
inside her head again. "I was just looking at your tie."

"Something wrong with it?"

"No. I imagine it's supremely correct." She sighed.
"I always feel so sorry for men in dark suits. They look
so... *joyless*."

"Joyless? Well, let me assure you I'm having the time
of my life." He surveyed her silently. "So you feel sorry
for elephants in zoos and men in dark suits."

She laughed. "That's right. Why don't you wear
something more colorful? Something with a little
pizzazz? Why don't you just say, 'Hey, to hell with what's
proper. I'm rich, I can do whatever I please.'"

A spark of humor glinted in his dark eyes. "I'll take
that suggestion under consideration." He wiped his
mouth with a paper napkin and came to his feet. He
was very tall and towered over her, looking down at her
as if he were ruling royalty. "And now, if you'll excuse
me, I'll be off."

An hour later, after all the boxes were packed, picked
up or delivered, Alicia went begging for a ride home.
Cousin Ramsey had taken off in his limo and left her
stranded.

The next morning Samantha heard the phone ring as she
was still outside on her way in with a load of firewood
for the stove. She dropped the logs on the porch and
rushed in to get the call. "Just let it ring, child," her
grandmother would have said. "If it's important they'll
call back." Samantha smiled as she reached for the
phone. It was one thing she could never do, let a phone

ring. Her curiosity simply could not stand it. Who could tell what wonderful surprises she would miss out on?

"Hello," she said, trying not to pant into the phone.

"Samantha Greene? This is Ramsey MacMillan."

At the sound of his deep voice, her heart made an unexpected leap in her chest. She took in a gulp of air. "Yes, Mr. MacMillan. Sorry, I'm out of breath. I heard the phone while I was outside, so I ran to catch it." She took in another deep breath. "What can I do for you?"

"I wonder if I could interest you in a ride in the country."

She glanced out the window at the wintry landscape. The trees were bare and the fields were dully green. The vague bluish shapes of the Blue Ridge Mountains loomed in the far distance. A ride in the country. She *lived* in the country, be it on the edge. Only a few miles from her house, new suburban developments sprawled in spick-and-span splendor.

"Why?" she asked.

"I would like your company."

He had to be kidding.

"Also, I would like to discuss your organization a little further. I understand you are the chairperson?"

"Yes, that's correct." If he wanted to talk about ACTION, she'd go. Anybody who wanted to talk about ACTION could have her time, and certainly someone who rode in a limo. "In that case, I'd love to go on a ride in the country, Mr. MacMillan," she said primly, smiling into the receiver.

"I'll be there in ten minutes." The line went dead.

Ten minutes? He must have been calling from the car. She glanced down at her faded jeans, decorated with heart-shaped knee patches, and the old red-and-blue tartan jacket that once had been her grandfather's. Well, it didn't really look like her grandfather's anymore. She'd cut the sleeves and knitted bright red cuffs and sewed them on, enlarged the buttonholes and added huge red buttons. It was the most comfortable, warm jacket she had. Maybe she should change her jeans into slacks, wear her dress coat. She threw the jacket onto a chair. Oh, Lord, she still had to put her makeup on too!

She rushed into the bathroom, washed her hands, put on eye shadow and mascara, then some lipstick. Taking out the rubber band, she shook her hair loose and brushed it out, leaving it to hang free over her shoulders. Once she'd dreamed of being a blue-eyed blonde, like Melissa, but that was a while ago. Now she was quite satisfied with her dark curly hair and hazel eyes, although she would have liked the addition of another inch or so to her height of five foot three. One more stroke of the brush and she was done. If all he had given her was ten minutes, he couldn't expect her to be all decked out like some glamour model. Besides, they were going for a ride. What did it matter? She ran into the bedroom and pulled off her old college sweatshirt and found a sweater, the one she'd just finished knitting copying an Italian design with vivid blues and greens.

The doorbell rang nine minutes after she'd put down the phone. She took a deep breath and went to answer it, her heart beating erratically.

"Good morning," he said, as she opened the door. In his dark pants, tweed jacket, shirt and tie, he looked less formal than the night before, but equally immaculate. There was also the very faint but exciting scent of some undoubtedly very expensive after-shave.

"Come in," she said. "I didn't get a chance to change, I mean..."

"No need to," he said, his gaze sweeping across the room, taking in the wall of books, the eclectic mixture of old and new furniture, the big wood stove, the bright cushions and curtains, the colourful Mexican rugs.

"It's the lived-in look," she said, watching him watch. "Not subject to the rules of decorating design, which makes it a very easy style to live with. Also, it doesn't ever get out of fashion, so you never have to worry about being behind the times and the laughingstock of the neighborhood. It's always correct, like the classics."

"I see," he said, his eyes resting on her face for a long moment, a smile lurking in his eyes.

Samantha had grown up in the small house, raised by loving grandparents. After their death a few years ago, the house had come to her. At one time she had been tempted to move away to a larger town, but she was glad she hadn't. She loved Aurora, Virginia. Her friends were here, she taught school here, and she liked living in the little house that was familiar and comfortable, and which she had decorated in her own nonconformist style.

"Are you ready?" he asked.

"Let me throw some more wood on the stove and turn it low." She opened the doors and shoved in two more logs, then closed the doors and turned the vents. "This will keep going for a while."

"You heat the house with this thing?"

"Yep. Works like a charm, too." She picked up her jacket and shoulder bag. "Oh, wait, let me show you something." She opened the door to one of the bedrooms. "This is the ACTION pantry."

All around the walls cheap metal shelves were stacked high with nonperishable foods. Ramsey scanned the room.

"Where does all this come from?"

"Churches mostly. Every month two churches are designated to collect food from their congregations. They bring it here. I put it on the shelves and put together the deliveries that are needed for the day. Volunteers pick them up here and deliver them. Anyway, if you ever find yourself without food to eat, you know where to call."

"Thank you," he said. "I'll remember that."

She moved back out of the room and closed the door behind her. "Shall we go?"

Alicia's silver Saab stood in the drive. "No limo?" she asked.

"I sent it back. I commandeered this one from Alicia. I stayed the night." He held the door open and she got in, then walked around the driver's side.

"I imagine you had no trouble commandeering it."

"None whatsoever."

"I suppose she told you where I live?"

"Right. In the little white fairy-tale house with the red trim five houses down from the school." He glanced down at the red hearts on her knees. "You like red."

"I do. It's my favorite color. It's bright and straight-forward and passionate."

"Like you?"

Samantha stared at him in surprise. "Like me? I hadn't thought about it that way." She looked out the window, embarrassed a little. Was that the way people saw her? Bright, straightforward and passionate? Well, there were worse things to be. She bit her lip to suppress a smile. Passionate. Well, most of her passion had been spent on her teaching job and her volunteer work with ACTION. It would be nice to spend some passion on a man, but a likely candidate had not presented himself lately.

"So what do you want?" Ramsey had asked her the night before. What she wanted was a man to love. Someone to share her life with. She was doing fine on her own, yet her life wasn't really complete. Something was missing. She wanted to be in love, hopelessly, help-lessly in love. She wanted to be married and have children and live happily ever after. A very old-fashioned dream, but then, in many ways, she was an old-fashioned woman.

"So tell me about ACTION," he said. "How does it work?"

"Hasn't Alicia told you?"

"I want to hear it from you."

She shrugged. "All right." She launched into her spiel, talking easily, as the car drove smoothly down the narrow country road. He asked her a few short questions and then remained silent after she had finished.

Samantha glanced out of the car window. She loved the country, the long winding roads with the beautiful farmhouses set back in the fields. Even in winter—ac-tually it was only late November and not officially winter yet—the scenery was beautiful with the dark evergreens silhouetted against the bright blue sky. She looked back at Ramsey's face. He had a classic profile, the Roman nose lending it character. She had the sudden urge to trace her finger down his nose, feel the bump. She liked the dark shine of his thick hair. It was the kind of hair you would like to run your fingers through. Probably not if it were sitting on Ramsey MacMillan's head, however. He did not seem the type who liked his hair mussed up. At least, not while he was out in public and driving a car. He might not mind at all in more intimate circumstances. An interesting thought.

What are you thinking about?

She straightened in her seat and put an end to her straying thoughts. "So," she said casually, "what do you do for a living?"

"I run the MacMillan Corporation."

"And what does that mean? What does the MacMillan Corporation do?" She had never heard of the MacMillan Corporation, but then she didn't read *Fortune* magazine or the *Wall Street Journal*.

He gave her a quick sideways glance. "It's a global engineering concern. We build bridges and dams and dikes and other massive structures the world over."

"Do you like it?"

His brows lifted in surprise. "Like it? I suppose I do."

"That's good. It must be terrible spending your life doing work you don't enjoy doing. I always wanted to be a teacher and a ballerina." She grinned. "Unfortunately, I couldn't do both, so I had to make a choice."

"And you're happy with the choice you made?"

"Oh, yes. I love teaching." She studied his face. "You didn't go for a ride just to talk about ACTION, did you?" she asked. Somehow she couldn't see him taking off on a leisurely drive in the country just for the beauty of it. It didn't fit the high-powered, ever-busy image of a business magnate, or whatever you called someone like him.

"Actually, no, but it was killing two birds with one stone. I have some business with a friend of mine who lives out past Middleburg. It's the kind that's better handled in person, but it won't take long, and in the meantime we could use the time to talk."

So they talked. Or rather, Samantha talked. Ramsey asked her brief questions and she gave him long answers. When she asked him a question he answered it with a minimum of words. He seemed not at all interested in talking about himself. There was something very reserved and aloof about him, and it triggered her curiosity.

The road curved sharply and he slowed down the car. "Well, here we are."

A sprawling estate appeared before her eyes, a magnificent historic plantation house set amid large formal gardens that must be a show to the eye in spring and summer.

"Oh," she said in awe as they drove up the long winding drive, "this is beautiful! He actually lives here?"

"Part of the year."

They got out of the car and walked up to the double front doors, which were opened before Ramsey had touched the large ornate brass knocker.

A servant showed them to a large sitting room resplendent with antique furniture and Oriental rugs and paintings on the wall that were no doubt original and priceless. The place looked like a museum, and Samantha glanced around practically holding her breath. Did people actually live in a place like this? A moment later a man and a woman entered the room.

The man, tall, very lean and graying, was wearing traditional riding clothes. The woman was much younger, in her late twenties perhaps, and wore a casual but deceptively elegant wool dress and high heels.

"Ramsey!" she exclaimed, coming forward with hands outstretched. "How wonderful to see you! It's been such a long time!" She touched her cheek to his and kissed the air.

Introductions were made. The twosome were father and daughter. The woman, Cecilia, gave Samantha a smile that was the phoniest she'd ever encountered. The pale blue eyes held a thinly veiled condescension as she quickly surveyed Samantha from top to bottom. Then, as if dismissing her, she abruptly looked back at Ramsey. "You are staying for lunch, are you?" she asked. "I forgot to ask you last night when we spoke on the phone, but we're counting on you."

"I don't want to inconvenience you," he said. "Richard and I only need about twenty minutes and we'll be out of your way."

"Nonsense! Come, let's have a drink, then lunch, and then you can talk."

He inclined his head. "All right, if you insist."

"We insist," Richard said. "Now, what shall it be?" He gave Samantha a questioning look.

She didn't feel like a drink in the middle of the day. "Actually, I'd love a cup of coffee if you have one handy."

"Of course, no problem at all. And you, Ramsey?"

"A glass of Evian, please."

Richard laughed. "Making sure you have a clear head for our little tête-à-tête?"

Ramsey smiled. "Always."

Ramsey wasn't drinking, but that didn't keep the other two from having a drink that looked decidedly less innocent than a glass of white wine. Cecilia had finished hers in a remarkably short time and poured herself another. It became obvious that she'd imbibed considerably before they'd even arrived. It was also obvious that she did not at all welcome Samantha, and it wasn't hard to guess why. Hostile vibrations sailed across the room.

Samantha straightened in her chair. She wasn't going to be intimidated by this rude woman, high heels or no.

Once at the table, things did not improve.

"We're having venison," Cecilia said to Ramsey. "Richard shot it himself two days ago."

"Bow and arrow," Richard added.

The hunting season for guns had not yet started. Samantha's grandfather had been an avid hunter and supplied their family with almost half of their need for meat every year. A delicacy in many places, venison had been on her plate regularly.

"Ever had venison?" Cecilia asked sweetly.

Samantha chewed her salad. "Yes, I have," she said, smiling nicely, determined not to let the woman get to her.

It was a delicious meal and Samantha enjoyed it thoroughly. She pretended not to notice Cecilia's little digs and barbs and reacted with polite pleasantry, aware of Ramsey's eyes observing her from across the table. Afterward, the men retired to Richard's study, leaving Samantha and Cecilia to their own devices. Samantha was not delighted at the prospect of spending the next twenty minutes or so in the company of this hostile woman with too much drink in her system.

"Well," Cecilia said, giving her the once-over, "where in the world did he pick you up?"

The question stunned Samantha, but not for long. She smiled. "On a grating in Washington, D.C.," she said. "I haven't had a bath in a month."

Cecilia gaped at her, apparently lost for words. Samantha took the opportunity to get up and leave the room. In the entry hall she found her jacket, pulled it on and went outside.

It was still cold, but the sun was shining. She took a deep breath of the crisp air and, looking up at the blue sky, she laughed out loud.

She'd wandered around the gardens for a while, then went back to the front of the house. She was freezing cold, but she wasn't going back inside. Maybe the car was open.

It was. She climbed inside and closed the door. The car was sitting in the shade of the house and the interior was only marginally less cold than the outside.

Time passed. Fifteen minutes, half an hour. She was getting colder and colder and angrier and angrier. What in hell did Ramsey MacMillan think he was doing? He'd invited her for a ride in the country to talk about ACTION, and here she was, acquiring frostbite, while he was conducting business, as if her time was worth nothing. As if she could just hang around waiting for His Majesty to be done. She climbed out of the car and started jumping up and down to get her blood flowing again. She could go back inside, of course, but she'd rather freeze first. Half an hour later he still was not back. Anger had changed into fury. Had the key been left in the ignition, she would have driven off.

She hunched deeper into her jacket and shivered. "Damn you, Ramsey MacMillan," she muttered, "you may have money and power and a limo, but you're arrogant and inconsiderate, and, as far as I'm concerned, the lions can have you!"

Ten minutes later she was about to go inside, find Richard's study, and demand to be taken home, when the front door opened and Ramsey emerged from the house. Gritting her teeth, Samantha watched him striding toward her.

He opened the car door, sat down in the driver's seat and gave her a probing look. "We were looking for you. What are you doing out in the cold?"

"The company's better out here," she said.

The front doors opened again and Richard came out and approached them. Holding on to the open car door, he bent over to see inside. "I see you found her." He smiled at Samantha. "It was good to see you both. We'll be here for the season. Stop by again."

"Thank you for lunch," Samantha said, smiling back. "The venison was delicious."

The civilities over, they drove off down the long drive, back to the road. She was too angry to speak and she stared out of the window, head turned away from Ramsey.

"How long were you out here?" he asked after a silence.

"Just about as long as you and Richard were in his study doing your royal business."

"We ran into some complications. We had to call Rome. I expected Cecilia would entertain you. What was the problem?"

She turned to face him. "Problem? How about problems—plural? Number one, you asked me for a ride in the country and I end up stranded in a fancy room full of antiques with a bitchy blonde full of liquor. Number two, you say you need to discuss business for twenty minutes or so, and leave me to my own devices. An hour and a half later, after I'm about frozen to death out here, you have the gall to ask me what the problem is. It may surprise you, but I have better things to do with my time than to play groupie and hang around waiting for you! Just because you're rich it doesn't mean you have the right to claim other people's time without any regard for their needs and feelings! I don't like to be used like that, not by you or anybody! You may have million-dollar deals to make, but I have wood to cut." She took a deep breath and clenched her teeth. So, she'd said it. She could probably say goodbye to the money. So be it. Maybe they'd be able to get funding from some other source.

He looked straight at the road. "I apologize."

He apologized. Boy, she was impressed.

"And number three, you should have told me we were going to see somebody. I could have changed out of these old jeans."

He glanced down at the heart-shaped patches on her knees. "I like your jeans."

"That's not the point."

"No. Again, I apologize. I had no idea you were sitting outside in the cold."

"That's not the point either."

"Right again. The point being, of course, that I was inconsiderate, selfish and arrogant."

"Self-knowledge is the beginning of all wisdom," she said sweetly. "My grandmother used to say that."

"I'll remember that. Now tell me what happened and why you were outside."

"Your inebriated admirer was being obnoxious, and I had no intention whatsoever of subjecting myself to that. I figured I'd take myself to the great outdoors and wait for you there. Twenty minutes is no big deal. An hour and a half was enough to freeze me to the bone."

"Are you still cold?"

"Yes."

"There's a little inn just down the road. We'll stop and have something hot to drink."

"Don't bother. I'll have something at home."

"We'll stop."

Yes, Your Majesty, she said silently.

The small inn-restaurant was located in a historic house with old-world charm and a cozy atmosphere. A fire crackled cheerfully in the fireplace.

"We'd like a table close by the fire," Ramsey said to the hostess, who looked as if she might be the proprietor. "Coffee?" he asked, looking at Samantha.

She nodded. "Anything to thaw me out."

"We have hot mulled wine," the lady said. "That ought to do the trick better than coffee."

"Oh, yes, wonderful!"

And it was. The hot spicy liquid flowed through her, warming her inside and out, mellowing her anger in the process. She stared at the fire, feeling the warmth of it. "Have you known her long? Cecilia, I mean."

"Years."

"She's after you."

"She's after my money," Ramsey said dryly.

"So am I."

His mouth curved in a crooked smile, but he said nothing, he just sat there and looked at her.

"For ACTION, that is," she modified. "That's why I came with you this morning." She should calm herself down, just on the remote chance he would still consider a donation.

"Of course."

Oh, damn, she thought, what a waste of time. "I'm not good at fund-raising, I suppose," she said.

"You're doing just fine."

She looked at him doubtfully. "A good fund-raiser knows how to suck up to people." Sucking up to people wasn't one of her strengths. Her mouth was too big; she talked too much.

"Not necessary." He leaned back in his chair and observed her calmly. "I have a proposition for you."

CHAPTER TWO

A PROPOSITION. Samantha stared at Ramsey. What did he mean by that? She took a sip of the warm wine. "What kind of proposition?" she queried.

He looked straight at her. "I'm willing to make a donation of five thousand dollars to ACTION."

Her heart began to race. Five thousand dollars! That was great, super, wonderful! It was all that, but it was not a proposition. She felt the stirrings of alarm.

"That's a very generous donation," she said carefully, "but I have the sneaking suspicion that something else is involved."

Ramsey's dark eyes were unreadable. "I have a number of obligations this holiday season, social as well as business, various functions to attend, and I would like you to make yourself available to accompany me."

She felt herself begin to gape and she closed her mouth. Why was he asking her? There had to be countless women fluttering around him, eager for his attentions. Gorgeous women with money and designer dresses. What did he want with her? It made no sense.

"You're joking," she said at last.

"No, I'm not joking."

"Why do you need me for that? There must be any number of women you could ask."

"So there are. I don't want them." It came out with finality.

She laughed. It was all too crazy to be real. "If you don't want to take any of the women you know, why not go alone?"

"It's not done. Besides, if I go alone I'll have the vultures descend on me."

She made a face. "Vultures?"

"For a man like me it's not a good idea to show up alone at these functions. It gives certain women the idea that they need to fill a supposed void in my life. And at the moment I simply don't want to deal with it."

"Oh, I see, how uncomfortable for you."

"Indescribable," he said with dry humor.

So he wanted her so she'd keep the vultures off his back. She was an unknown, a simple teacher who would not get any fancy notions or threaten his peace of mind. In the right clothes she'd be presentable, and she could speak in complete sentences. She wasn't a beauty queen, but she was nice enough to look at.

She met his eyes. "Vultures such as Cecilia, perchance?"

"Yes."

She held his gaze. "This little excursion into the countryside was a test, wasn't it?"

His mouth twitched. "Of course."

A few unfriendly thoughts entered her head, but she contained them. She twisted the stem of her glass between her fingers. "I like your donation of five thousand dollars. But my going out with you to fancy functions is a crazy idea," she said slowly. "I've never been to that kind of affair. I wouldn't know what to talk about. I haven't got any clothes for that sort of occasion."

Ramsey made a dismissive gesture. "Naturally I'll take care of all your expenses—clothes, shoes, accessories, whatever. Consider them business expenses."

Naturally. Samantha bit her lip. "I don't believe this."

"Why not? It's a simple business deal. I want to buy your time."

Was she being naive? she wondered, sipping the rest of her wine. Did she perhaps not quite grasp the implications of such an offer? She wasn't sure how this type of setup worked in the higher echelons of society. "And all I have to do is dress up in sequins and attend these affairs with you?"

"Right."

"And after the event is over, you'll take me back home?"

"That will be inconvenient—often these affairs last till late." His voice was cool, businesslike. "Unless you have to teach the next day, you'll be my guest at my apartment."

Her heart sank. "I was afraid of that."

His face gave nothing away. "I'll have a room prepared for you. You'll be quite comfortable."

"I don't doubt it for a minute. But if you expect me to sleep with you, you can forget it. There's no way in the world I'm going to jump into bed with you, so if you..."

One dark brow raised in amused surprise, and she felt the heat of embarrassment rush into her cheeks.

He gave her a long look. "Am I that unappetizing a fellow?"

No, he wasn't. As a matter of fact, she was scared to death of his male appeal. For some dark and hidden reason, she was intrigued by his calm, controlled manner. It challenged her: it made her want to break through it.

She swallowed hard. "That's not what I meant. I just..."

"I know. Well, let me be perfectly clear. This is a business proposition, with no sexual duties included."

She straightened and lifted her chin. "Will you commit that to paper?"

His face revealed no emotion. "If you want to."

"I want to." Samantha didn't know if it would mean anything legally, but she certainly didn't want him to think she was stupid and gullible.

Ramsey came to his feet. "Let me get my briefcase from the car and we'll handle it right now. You can look it over and see if it's to your satisfaction."

He strode out and was back a minute later carrying a leather briefcase. Opening it, he found paper and pen and began to write. He had beautiful hands, tanned, with strong, lean fingers, square nails and no rings. Sexy hands. She wondered how it would feel to be touched

by these hands—to be stroked gently, sensuously... She
jerked upright in her chair and took a gulp of her wine.
Good Lord, she must be losing her mind! She'd just told
him there was no way she was going to go to bed with
him and here she sat, fantasizing about his hands
touching her while he was committing the purity of his
intentions to paper.

He capped his pen. "Here you go." He handed her
the paper.

She read the words written in big, bold handwriting,
and it was right there, black on white, exactly as he had
said. Only ACTION was not mentioned, neither the
amount of the donation. Maybe it was just as well to
keep it out.

"How much money did you say again?" she queried.

"Five thousand plus expenses."

She nodded thoughtfully. "How rich are you? I mean,
just run-of-the-mill kind of rich, real rich, filthy rich or
obscene rich?"

He gave a crooked little smile. "For somebody who
doesn't seem to care much about money, you're showing
quite an interest."

"Oh, I care plenty for money, don't make a mistake
about it. I want ten thousand." Her heart pounded so
loud that she was worried he might hear it, or the rest
of the people in the restaurant.

His face didn't move a muscle. "You drive a hard
bargain."

She smiled. "I'm a tough cookie. And you're asking
quite a lot of me." The thought of mingling with the
rich and famous held a certain appeal. It also held an
undeniable terror. She was a good teacher, she was a
good organizer, she knew how to cook and sew and knit
and chop wood and she read the newspaper every day.
Socializing with the crème de la crème was not one of
her talents.

Ramsey observed her calmly. "I'll give you eight, with
the understanding that during the school vacation you'll
stay in town during the day when I need you."

"Need me for what?"

"Business lunches, whatever comes up."

His crisp tone irked her, as if he assumed she had all the time in the world to give to him. "I do have a life of my own, you know. The food pantry is in my house. Somebody needs to put together the daily deliveries. We have to make up special food deliveries for Christmas meals, like we did for Thanksgiving. I should be available to take care of any emergency situations that come up." She put her hands up in the air and dropped them. "I can't just put everything on hold."

"Make arrangements, work around it." He shrugged.

Of course. It was simple. Make arrangements, he said. Of course, that was the way it worked for him. If you had money you could make arrangements for anything. You could order people around, you could make demands. Being rich made you powerful and influential.

"Don't look at me like that," he said. "Get call forwarding on your phone line and transfer the calls to come in to my number. I'll get an answering service to handle them when you're out. Then, when it's necessary for you to go home, work it into the schedule. I imagine you'll have plenty of time."

It sounded reasonable enough. For eight thousand dollars she ought to be able to figure something out. Eight thousand dollars was worth a few sacrifices.

She nodded. "All right then, I accept, but Christmas Eve and Christmas Day I'm spending with my friend Melissa and her family." They'd been best friends since kindergarten. Melissa's family was like her own.

"No problem."

"There's one more condition," she said. "I want you to make a straight donation to ACTION and promise me not to ever, *ever* mention this arrangement we've made. Not to anybody. Please."

He nodded. "It's a deal. Now, the first event will be next week Saturday—a benefit dinner."

Next week Saturday. Samantha's heart sank. She was going to be in Philadelphia with Paul and Lee Ann for the holiday weekend. Well, she'd just have to come back Saturday morning instead of Sunday. It was too late now to change her mind.

"A benefit dinner?" she queried. "Is that one of those affairs where they charge two hundred and fifty dollars per plate and everybody shows up in sequins and feathers?"

"Five hundred per plate," he corrected. "And yes, it is one of those affairs, a fund-raiser for a new museum."

"The food must be wonderful."

"Not necessarily," he said dryly. "I can't promise a thing." He took a checkbook out of his briefcase and began to write. "Four thousand now, and the other four on January the first." He began to write a second check. "And this is for expenses. Get yourself a dress, shoes, whatever you need. Formal." He looked up for a moment. "If you need help, ask Alicia. Go easy on feathers and sequins. Remember the classics—they're always correct."

"Yessir," she said, feeling like saluting.

The wine finished, they got back into the car. Despite the cold, it was a gorgeous, sunny afternoon, and it seemed even brighter now with the prospect of Ramsey MacMillan's donation to ACTION. Elation bubbled up inside her and she felt like laughing out loud.

They crossed a tiny rustic bridge over a narrow, bubbling stream. On the other side, by the road, two teenagers in jeans and parkas were sitting on a fallen tree trunk, kissing passionately, oblivious of the world around them and the freezing temperature.

"Ah, young love," said Samantha, and sighed theatrically.

"They'll get frostbite," said Ramsey.

She laughed, tossing her hair back over her shoulder. "No way. They don't even feel the cold."

"Speak from experience?"

She grinned. "Of course. I was in love dozens of times as a teenager. Even longer than a week sometimes."

"Sounds serious," he said.

"I *was* serious, at the time. I always thought it was real, until it was over, and then I wondered how I could have fooled myself so easily." She sighed. "I grew out of it."

"Out of what?"

"Falling in love all the time all over the place."

"So what then?"

"I fell in love for real. When I was twenty-two, in college. It lasted more than a year."

"Then what?"

"I found out he had a girlfriend in his hometown, planning a wedding."

One dark brow raised in question. "What happened after you found out?"

"He said he'd cancel the wedding. I said no, thank you."

She'd felt devastated and disillusioned, and angry that she hadn't seen through his deception.

"And after that?"

"I hated all men, of course. For about six months. I couldn't keep it up, though. It took too much energy, you know. Besides, it didn't seem quite fair to mistrust half of the human race because one man had treated me so shabbily. Also, I've got plenty of good friends I know well, men who are perfectly trustworthy." She grinned. "The problem is, I'm not in love with them. Too bad. So here I am, twenty-six, a spinster schoolteacher. Sad, isn't it?"

He nodded. "Tragic. Would you like to be married?"

"Yes, but only to the right man, otherwise it isn't worth the trouble. So what about your love life? You must have known some very rich, glamorous women." She couldn't believe she was actually asking him that. But then she'd told him about hers; it was his turn.

"My reputation has been wildly exaggerated," he assured her.

It was all he said, and she knew better than to ask more.

Entering Leesburg, they found their path blocked by a truck full of construction material trying to negotiate a turn into a narrow driveway leading up to an old Colonial house with a sagging porch and peeling paint.

"It's the Foley house!" Samantha exclaimed. "It's finally being fixed up!"

Ramsey glanced at the house. "Looks like it needs it."

"I know. It's a shame to see such a beautiful place get so dilapidated. I mean, there's history there, and those old houses have so much character."

They waited. The truck was not doing well. "Somebody must have bought it," Samantha said. "They must be in a hurry if they're having people work on it on a Saturday. It's going to cost a fortune to get that place back into shape." She sighed. "I'd love to see what it looks like inside when it's all fixed up." She glanced at Ramsey. "What kind of a place do you live in?"

"I live in an apartment in Washington. I have a house, but it's too big for just me and I only use it on occasion."

The truck was lumbering up the driveway now, and Ramsey accelerated and continued down the road, past the other old houses, farther into the old historic town with its narrow streets and small shops.

Past Leesburg, a long winding country road led them back to Aurora, which was nothing more than a crossroads village with about eighty houses, a gas station, a small general store, a tiny church and the elementary school.

"Did you grow up here?" he asked.

Samantha nodded. "Yes. My grandparents raised me. And Paul did too, in a manner of speaking. He's my uncle, actually, but he's more like a brother. He's only twelve years older than I am. He lives in Philadelphia now with Lee Ann, his wife, and their twin daughters. I'm going there for Thanksgiving." She made a face. "Sorry if I bore you. You didn't ask for my life story."

"There must be more to your life story than that."

"Oh, not much. I'm excruciatingly ordinary."

He gave her a quick sideways glance, but said nothing. He drove up the short drive and stopped in front of her small house. He opened the car door for her, and she climbed out.

He was standing close, towering over her, and she had to look up to see his face. His dark eyes locked with hers and she felt a strange, fluttering sensation in her stomach.

"So we have a deal," he stated, extending a big tanned hand.

She put her hand in his and looked into his eyes. "Yes." It was hard to keep her face straight and businesslike. She had a terrible urge to laugh, and as she looked into his eyes she saw the challenge there.

She composed herself. "And thank you for the donation," she said politely. "The money will make a big difference."

"Good. I'll see you next week. I'll call you." He released her hand.

She went inside and, looking through the window, watched him ease his tall, lean body into the driver's seat.

It wasn't until then that panic hit her.

Oh, God, what had she got herself into now?

CHAPTER THREE

SAMANTHA did not sleep well that night, her mind wild with worries. Her dreams were confused, with images of Ramsey in shirtsleeves, his dark eyes looking deep into hers. She ran her hands through his hair. It was very thick and silky. "You have very sexy hair," she whispered in his ear, then he put his arms around her and kissed her.

"I know you want to sleep with me," he murmured. "All women do. Do you like silk sheets?"

But the silk sheets were very cold. "I like flannel in the winter," she said.

She awoke, freezing cold, the quilt on the floor. She covered herself up and fell asleep again, but her sleep was no more restful. She awoke feeling wrung out.

"You won't believe what happened," she said to Melissa later that day. She'd been invited for Sunday dinner at Melissa's parents' house and they were alone in the kitchen, fixing the salad.

Samantha told Melissa what had transpired the day before, and Melissa listened, blue eyes wide with disbelief, elation, and excitement.

"Imagine!" she said. "You'll be jet-setting! Think of all those gorgeous clothes you'll need! Think of the money for ACTION!"

Samantha grimaced. "The money I can handle. The jet-setting I'm not so sure about." It felt good to be able to confide in someone, and she was glad Melissa didn't seem to think she'd been crazy to accept Ramsey's offer.

"I wish I could go with you to shop for a dress," Melissa said regretfully, "but I'm still on the three-to-eleven shift this week." Melissa was a nurse and worked at the hospital in Leesburg. "Why don't you ask Alicia?"

36

"She has friends from Italy staying at her house, remember? I don't even want to ask her and put her on the spot. Lee Ann will go with me on Friday, in Philadelphia."

That night Samantha didn't sleep any better than the previous one, tossing and turning and dreaming of Ramsey.

The morning was cold and colorless. She dragged herself out of bed. She was still dragging by the time she stood in front of the classroom, looking at twenty-three small faces.

"On Thursday it's Thanksgiving," she said. "Who knows why we celebrate Thanksgiving?" Several eager hands went up.

"'Cause the Pilgrims did, and they invited the Indians and had a party."

"The Pilgrims came from England," Kirstin said primly. She stood up, regal as a little princess. "They brought seeds and food with them on the boats. When they got to America they planted food and the Indians helped them a lot. Then when the food was ready they had a celebration because they were very thankful for all the food. They ate turkey and corn and yams and pumpkin pie. And that's why we still have Thanksgiving, 'cause we should be grateful for having food and stuff." She sat down, looking triumphant.

"Very good, Kirstin," Samantha said. "The Pilgrims came to America hundreds of years ago. They were the first settlers. Do you think it was easy or difficult to live in a new country?"

The day went on. Despite the fact that she was busy and the kids claimed her attention practically every minute of the day, thoughts of Ramsey MacMillan kept slipping into her mind. She kept seeing his face, and shivers of fearful excitement ran through her more than once. She kept thinking about having to buy a dress. Not just any dress, but an evening gown, special and expensive. The check Ramsey had given her was a clear indication what he expected, and it wasn't a party dress from a discount store.

On Wednesday after school she climbed in her little red Toyota and made for Philadelphia to spend Thanksgiving with Paul, Lee Ann and the twins. She couldn't wait to tell Lee Ann about Ramsey MacMillan.

Lee Ann was practically speechless, then she laughed. "We'll go shopping for a dress on Friday!"

"Oh, Lee Ann, thanks. I hoped you'd say that." Samantha made a face. "Do you think it was crazy, what I did?"

"For all that money for ACTION? Of course not. Just as long as you're sure the guy isn't some high-class swindler."

Paul, the lawyer, was less enthusiastic. "Let me check up on this guy before you do anything, Sam. Let me make a few phone calls."

The phone calls generated nothing but excellent references, and Paul, coming out of his study, looking stunned.

"Sam," he said, "he's one of the wealthiest men on the East Coast! Wherever did you meet him?"

"In the school cafeteria," she answered promptly.

All Thursday morning Samantha and Lee Ann were busy preparing the turkey dinner. It was a warm and wonderful holiday, as it always was when she spent it with Paul and his family.

On Friday morning, Lee Ann drove them into town. "I know just the place to go," she said. "Wait till you see it."

The shop window was overwhelming. Tall, slender mannequins draped in silks and satins looked disdainfully down on the lusting mortals gaping at them.

"I've never been in a place like this," Samantha whispered. "Even the mannequins look arrogant!" She glanced at Lee Ann and a laugh escaped her. "Suppose they'll let us in?"

"It's a free country, and my husband's a lawyer." Without further ado, Lee Ann took the polished brass rail of the glass door, opened it and pushed Samantha in ahead of her.

A saleslady sheathed in mauve silk came rushing over. "Ladies, may I help you?" Her face was decorated with glamour makeup and she looked like the mannequins in the shop window.

Samantha lifted her chin and smiled. "I need a dress," she said. "I'm going to a very fancy dinner on Saturday."

"I see," said the saleslady, with an obvious lack of enthusiasm.

"It's in D.C., a fund-raising affair," Samantha elaborated. "The one everybody's going to. I need something formal, but not boring, please."

The lady looked at her suspiciously, taking in her appearance, which was perfectly respectable, but not exactly designer status.

Samantha smiled sweetly, succumbing to the little devil inside her once more. "I know I don't look it, but I've got tons of money, don't worry."

The saleslady looked aghast, then quickly recovered. "Well, let's see. Have you any particular designer in mind?"

Designer. Oh, dear. "No, but I'm always interested in the new and upcoming ones. Fresh ideas, lots of creativity. You know what I mean." Samantha smiled brightly.

"Of course," said the lady, "let me see." She gave Samantha a calculating look. "Size eight?"

Samantha nodded, watching the lady move over to one of the racks and produce a shimmering black creation.

"How about something like this? It's very elegant, and black is always right."

"It's beautiful," Lee Ann said, fingering the fabric.

"I hate it," Samantha said. "It's like something you'd wear to a funeral."

The saleslady's eyes widened. "Black is very elegant, very *chic*, as the French say."

"I know what the French say. Black is morbid. I want something with color."

So the lady brought something with color. Ruby red, emerald green, turquoise green, topaz blue. Samantha smiled brightly. "That's more like it."

The woman did not approve of her, she was quite aware of it. It gave her a secret satisfaction. It tickled the little devil inside her.

It took them several hours and several shops to find the dress Samantha liked, a long green and gold gown of shimmering silk. It fitted her perfectly, and she loved the sensuous feel of the silk swirling around her legs as she moved.

The price was astronomical.

"It's not too expensive," Lee Ann argued, as she had done all morning. "He didn't give you all this money to buy a bargain basement dress. He intended for you to do it up grand. You'll have to look great, you know that. Think of all the other people there—famous artists, politicians, oil magnates, movie stars, Russian counts. Just think of what the women will be wearing."

"I feel unreal. Look at me! I've never worn anything as elegant as this!" Samantha protested.

"You look gorgeous."

"It doesn't look like me."

"Because you're not used to seeing yourself this way. You're used to comfortable, casual things, spending your time with kids all day. But you really look fabulous in this. You've got a great body, so show it off. Walk that ballerina walk of yours." Lee Ann sighed enviously. "I wish I'd done ballet as a kid. Would have done wonders for my posture."

"Just stand up straight," said Samantha.

Lee Ann rolled her eyes. "Spare me, Sam. I know how it's done. It's just not second nature, as it is for you. I noticed it the first time I came home with Paul. I watched you walk across the lawn. You were eleven or something and there wasn't anything awkward about you. You moved like a dancer, fluid and easy, and full of confidence. And that at the age of eleven, for Pete's sake."

"If I decide to take the dress, will you shut up?"

Lee Ann grinned. "Yes."

"It's a deal."

It took them several more hours to find the right shoes, stockings and evening bag to match, everything Samantha needed, except jewelry and a stole.

"You can borrow my grandmother's necklace and earrings," Lee Ann offered. "The ones with the emeralds—they'll be perfect with your dress. And I have a black velvet stole you can use."

"Oh, Lee Ann, I can't do that!"

"Sure you can—I insist. The emeralds are insured, so don't worry."

Still uncertain, Samantha accepted. It was, after all, a day for uncertainties and new adventures. She'd never spent so much money in one day in her entire life. She'd never spent so much money on a single dress. There was something completely unreal about it. It was a good thing Lee Ann was with her or she would never had had the courage to go through with her purchases.

"I've been thinking," Lee Ann said as they were driving back home. "You'll be spending quite a bit of time with this man, and..." She frowned. "You'll be careful, won't you, Sam? I don't want to see you get hurt."

"Careful? I told you about the paper. He's not looking for anything sexual—that's the whole point. He..."

"That's not what I mean. What I mean is...oh, hell, just don't fall in love with the guy, Sam."

Samantha stared at Lee Ann and the dream came back to her with full force. She took a deep breath.

"I'm not going to. I'm not stupid, Lee Ann. It's only a business arrangement. I have absolutely no illusions."

"Falling in love is not a conscious decision, Sam."

"Well, then I have to make it a conscious decision not to."

Lee Ann looked doubtful. "He's handsome, he's rich, he'll take you to all kinds of glamorous places and events. It's powerful stuff, Sam."

"I know that. But I'm a very practical, down-to-earth schoolteacher. Don't worry about me." Samantha sounded a lot more certain than she felt.

What she really felt was a sense of unease.

What if she did fall in love?

Well, she wasn't going to. It was as simple as that.

Ramsey called soon after she'd returned home the next day, and again his voice had the strangest effect on her. She could see him in her mind's eye as if he were standing in the room, see his dark eyes, his thick hair, the cool, aloof expression on his face. She saw his hands holding the phone.

"Samantha?" His voice was terse. "Are you there?"

"Yes, yes." She swallowed.

"I'm calling to check if you found what you needed for tonight, or if there's anything else you need."

"Oh, no, I'm ready."

"Good. I'll send the car for you. Simon will bring you over here, so you can change. Four-thirty suit you?"

"That'll be fine."

"I'll see you later, then."

The limousine arrived exactly at four-thirty as promised. Standing at her bedroom window, Samantha saw the car drive up and watched the chauffeur walk up to the door. The bell rang. She picked up her overnight bag, draped the dress in its protective covering over her arm and went to answer the door.

The chauffeur, resplendent in uniform, greeted her, then took her things and helped her into the back. He was tall and thin, and looked very proper.

"Help yourself to whatever you like," he said, pointing to a drinks cabinet. "There's coffee in this cabinet. If you need to speak to me just push this button.''

''Thank you.'' It was all she could manage to say for the moment. The man closed the door and a moment later they moved noiselessly down the road.

She surveyed her surroundings. This was not a car; this was a room on wheels. The seats were large and comfortable. There was a TV set, a telephone, and a cabinet that contained all manner of bottles, ice, and glasses. Below the window was a magazine rack which held magazines and newspapers, all current. She bit her lip to stifle a laugh. Oh, boy, Melissa, I wish you could see me now, she thought.

A small cabinet held a vacuum coffeepot, sugar, cream, and a small box with a gold bow on top. ''Dalloyau, Paris,'' it said. Inside were half a dozen exquisite small pastries, like pieces of art. Samantha felt a sudden irrepressible urge to giggle—nerves, she knew. Fresh pastries from Paris! Was he trying to impress her? Well, he had succeeded: she was impressed. She picked up the lovely china coffee cup and turned it over. Wedgwood. She didn't know much about china, but she'd heard about Wedgwood. She set it back down on its saucer. Oh, dear Lord, would she dare drink from it? Maybe what she needed was a drink instead to calm her nerves.

No, she'd rather have coffee. She poured it carefully in the cup and examined the pastries again. They looked mouth-wateringly delicious and much too beautiful to eat. Well, she would force herself.

Darkness had fallen by the time they reached the Washington apartment complex. A uniformed man came out of the building as soon as the limo stopped in front.

''Miss Greene?'' he asked as he helped her from the car.

''Yes.''

''Mr. MacMillan is expecting you. Please follow me.''

''My things...'' she began.

''Don't worry, they'll be sent right up.''

She followed him in, her heart beating nervously. The lobby was plush—glimmering with shiny brass and glittering crystal chandeliers. The man ushered her into a waiting elevator, which seemed rather small for such a large building, until it dawned on her that it was probably a private one. They zoomed almost noiselessly to the top floor, where the door swished open to expose a small entryway with large double doors which opened almost immediately. Her heart lurched.

Dressed in dark suit pants, shirt and waistcoat, the jacket discarded, Ramsey looked down at her.

"Hello, Samantha," he said. "Come in." His gaze turned to the man who had come with her. "Thank you, Nick."

The man inclined his head. "The lady's luggage will be here in a moment," he said as he stepped back into the elevator.

Samantha gazed in awe at the interior of the apartment. All she could see was another entryway with a marble floor, a large antique bevelled mirror that reached from floor to ceiling, a high table carved with Chinese designs along the sides and legs displaying an opulent arrangement of exotic fresh flowers.

She stood by the door, afraid to put a foot inside lest she should mar the perfection. What if her shoes were dirty, or she knocked something over?

"Are you coming in or not?" asked Ramsey.

"Just a minute." She bent down and pulled at the laces of her ankle boots and slipped out of them. Looking up, she saw his amused surprise and lifted her chin. "No sense in making things dirty. My shoes come straight from the country."

"Of course. Come along."

Before she had moved a few steps over the cold marble floor, a small dark-haired woman appeared out of nowhere.

"I'm sorry, Mr. MacMillan, I didn't hear the bell."

"It didn't ring, Mrs. Gregory." Ramsey turned to Samantha. "This is Mrs. Gregory, who runs the place and takes care that I don't starve to death. Mrs. Gregory, this is Samantha Greene. She'll be here off and on during the holiday season.''

Samantha smiled and extended her hand. Mrs. Gregory took it and looked at her suspiciously, then smiled back, as if something had reassured her. ''Mr. MacMillan told me you were coming. I'll show you to your room.''

The bell rang and Mrs. Gregory hastened to open the door.

''My things,'' Samantha said. She bit her lip, suddenly assailed with new doubt. ''I hope I bought the right kind of dress.''

Ramsey took her elbow and ushered her into the living room. ''Don't worry about it.''

Well, if he wasn't, why should she?

She forgot about the dress instantly. In front of her were floor-to-ceiling windows with a panoramic view of the Potomac river and the city sparkling with lights.

''Oh, wow,'' she said with a sigh. ''This is gorgeous!'' She moved on her socked feet across the thick Chinese carpets to stand closer by the windows. ''I've never seen the city this way.'' She turned and looked around. The room had a distinct Far Eastern flavor with its large Chinese carpet, the low carved wooden coffee table and huge palms in blue and white Oriental pots positioned on low carved stands. Utterly fascinated, her gaze swept from object to object, paintings, carvings, sculptures, all of them exquisite and interesting. She looked up suddenly, aware that Ramsey was watching her.

''Sorry,'' she said. ''I suppose it's not good manners to be so curious, but it's all very beautiful.''

''Look all you want.'' He shrugged. ''I don't mind.''

Mrs. Gregory came back to take her to her room, which, too, was sumptuous. Thick carpeting, a large bed with a quilted silk cover with a design of exotic birds and flowers and matching draperies, a private bathroom with a whirlpool bath and expensive bath products on the shelves. Samantha ran her hand over the thick, lush

towels. They were warm, and she laughed. They were
hanging over a heated rail. Oh, good heavens, what
luxury! Huge mirrors. Enormous cupboards with special
compartments for shoes and drawers and shelves, all
cedar. She looked at her watch. Plenty of time for a
bath. She raised her arms above her head, pirouetted,
laughing softly, then turned on the water and poured in
some bath salts that smelled heavenly.

She didn't stay in too long, afraid it might take longer
than she was expecting to get ready.

Two bathrobes hung behind the door, one soft pink,
the other a beautiful deep jade green. She took the green
one off the hook and slipped it on. It was too big, but
it felt good. She wrapped a dry towel around her head
and moved back into the bedroom, the bathrobe softly
sweeping over the carpeting.

A knock on the door startled her.

"Who is it?" she called.

"Just me. Are you decent?"

She chuckled. "Very." She opened the door.

Ramsey held a large velvet box in his hand. "Alicia
suggested you might need some jewelry. These are some
things my mother left in the safe. Have a look and see
if you can use any of them. Otherwise, we'll find something else."

She took the box from him. "I have jewelry for tonight," she said. "I borrowed it." She opened the box
and stared. It looked like a burglar's cache—necklaces,
earrings, bracelets, all neatly arranged on black velvet.
Gleaming gold, glittering diamonds, precious stones of
various colors and sizes. She took a deep breath.

"I'm not sure I'll feel comfortable wearing your
mother's jewelry."

"She probably doesn't even know she has it. It's been
in the safe for God knows how many years. The things
she cares about she has with her in Hawaii."

"What if I lose something?" she queried.

"It's all insured, and I've had everything cleaned and
checked to make sure nothing is loose or broken. You
have nothing to worry about."

Samantha closed the box. She had no choice. It was all part of this little dress-up game, part of the costume she needed for the play.

"Where should I keep it?" she asked.

"I'll put it in the safe in my study. I'll get it out when you're here."

"All right, then." She handed him the box. "I'll wear what Lee Ann loaned me tonight."

"Fine." He took the box from her. "Would you care for a drink or something to eat while you're getting ready? It will be late before we eat."

"Oh. Well, yes—a drink, I mean. I'm not hungry. I ate three of the pastries in the limo. I was a glutton."

"They were there to be eaten," he said levelly.

"Where did you find them? I mean, the box said..."

"I flew them in."

"Oh." Of course, how silly of her to ask.

"I was in Paris yesterday for a meeting," he explained. "I thought you might like them."

"Oh, I did." She smiled. "They were sinfully delicious." He had thought she'd like them. He'd been in Paris, just for a meeting, mind you, and he'd been thinking about her. It was an exciting thought.

"You have your own plane?" she asked.

"The company has several." His gaze skimmed over her. "You'll find that the pink robe will be more your size."

"I don't like pink. It's much too sweet."

Humor glimmered in his eyes. "Of course. Doesn't fit your personality. Red and passionate is more your style."

She could feel the color creep into her face. Oh, damn, she thought, wishing she'd never made that comment about red being passionate. Composing herself, she shrugged casually. "I just like bright colors."

"Well," he said then, "let me get you that drink. What would you like?"

"Oh, anything. Something interesting. Surprise me."

"As long as it's not sweet and pink, I take it. Be right back."

Samantha sat down on the stool in front of the dressing table, put moisturizer on her face and began to towel her hair. There was a bouquet of white roses on the dressing table, and a collection of small bottles of perfume—Joy, Chanel Number 5, Gucci, and several others. A small fortune captured in crystal.

A few moments later Ramsey came back with a cocktail glass with a bright red drink containing a cherry and a slice of lemon. "Here you go," he said, face impassive.

"Thank you," she said politely. Damn the man and his red drink. She took a careful sip. It was a potent mixture with no flavor she recognized, but it was delicious. "What is this?" she asked. "What's in it?"

"My own concoction. It has red vermouth in it."

She felt the little devil stirring inside her. "I bought a red dress—crimson, very tight, with lots of ruffles and flounces. A little carnivalish."

"Is that right?" His face gave nothing away.

Well, what had she expected? That he'd blow up in anger? Hardly. He was too composed for that. His eyes held hers and she bit her lip, trying not to laugh.

His mouth quirked. "You're not a very good liar, Samantha."

"Well, I almost did." She grinned, she couldn't help it. "Then I thought it might be just a little too... flamboyant. Not classic enough."

"So you got a little black dress."

"I wouldn't sink that deep. It's green." She jumped up. "Let me show you."

He held up his hand. "I'd prefer to see it with you in it. I'll wait. Surprise me." He moved to the door. "Enjoy your drink."

She frowned at the closed door, wondering suddenly why he had come to her himself with the drink rather than giving instructions to Mrs. Gregory. She shrugged. It wasn't likely she would figure this man out. She might as well save herself the effort. She looked at herself in the mirror.

You *want* to figure him out.

No, I don't.

You'd love to know what's hiding behind that glimmer in those dark eyes. What passions stir inside his heart— *Oh, stop it!*

She took a deep breath and took a drink from her glass. Then she opened the bottles of perfume and smelled them one after the other. Maybe she should use Chanel Number 5. It would be safe—and classic. Definitely supremely classic. She grimaced at herself in the mirror. Probably every other woman at the dinner tonight would be wearing it.

She felt a stirring of rebellion. Ramsey was buying her clothes and shoes and hose and evening bags. He was giving her his mother's jewelry to wear. She was all decked out with his money; she could at least wear her own perfume.

She took out the bottle of L'Air du Temps and dabbed some behind her ears, on her wrists and throat and a little between her breasts. The bottle said *au de parfum*, which was a less potent version of the actual perfume, but she liked it that way. Also it was not nearly as expensive.

As she put on her makeup and fixed her hair on top of her head, she wondered about the evening ahead and the people she would meet. It was a rather daunting prospect to be in the company of a roomful of rich, famous and powerful people. How was she going to hold her own in conversation? She had no idea what high society in Washington talked about apart from the obvious: politics, the arts, business, all subjects in which she was not particularly well versed.

Maybe she should say she wasn't up to date on the latest in-gossip because she'd been out of the country for the last two years.

Then they'd ask where.

She could say Brazil, or Australia, but that would be dangerous. They might know all about Brazil or Australia.

She could say she'd spent the last two years in a convent in the south of Italy. Oh, no, it would never work. She grimaced at her reflection in the mirror. She'd just have to fake it somehow. Perhaps she could do something revolutionary: Tell the truth. I'm a first-grade teacher in Aurora, Virginia, and I'm afraid I don't know much about this. After all, what was wrong with being a teacher? It was a perfectly respectable profession, if not a lucrative one.

Carefully she slipped the dress over her head. It fitted her beautifully, and the green was luscious and rich. Lee Ann's emeralds were a perfect match.

She stared at herself in the mirror. With her hair up, the emeralds around her neck, and her dress softly draping around her body, she looked wonderful. She felt wonderful. She took a deep breath. If only Ramsey thought she looked wonderful. After all, he was the one who would be seen with her in public. What a risk he was taking! What if she really had bought a red carnival dress? If he appeared with a hideously dressed woman at his side, he'd have to suffer the long-term consequences. She was going to be safely ensconced in the Virginia countryside after all this was over. Well, she was not hideously dressed. At least, after all the money she'd spent, she sure hoped not.

She picked up her evening bag and Lee Ann's velvet stole. Taking a deep breath, she opened the door and walked down the hall into the living room with her ballerina walk, as Lee Ann had suggested. He was sitting in a chair, dressed in evening clothes, reading the *Wall Street Journal*. She could feel her heart thump against her ribs when he looked up and saw her. She stood still and tilted her chin.

"I'm ready," she said.

CHAPTER FOUR

THERE was a silence as Ramsey's dark gaze slowly moved over Samantha. "You look beautiful," he said quietly. "Quite beautiful."

"Thank you." Her pulse leaped and she clutched her evening bag in her hands, willing herself to relax.

He came to his feet. "Ready, then?"

Samantha nodded. He looked magnificent. She liked the looks of the bow tie, the elegance of the dinner jacket with its silk collar. She liked the way his dark eyes were looking at her, sending tingles of excitement down her spine.

"It's cold outside," he said. "Let me help you with your stole." Taking it from her, he draped it around her shoulders. There was a gentle brush of his warm hand against her bare skin, then the sensuous softness of the velvet. Brown eyes looking into hers. Silk swirling around her legs. Her heart was racing.

She swallowed. "Thank you."

He held the door open for her and she preceded him out. They went down in the elevator and she willed her heart to calm its nervous rhythm. You're going nuts, she told herself. A silk dress, a velvet stole, brown eyes and his hand touching you, and you're floating.

It must be the drink. Maybe he put a secret ingredient in it that made me lose my head.

Get yourself together. The evening hasn't even started yet.

Uneasily, she surveyed herself in the mirrored panels. She looked like a stranger to herself. She *felt* like a stranger. Even her reaction to his touch was out of the ordinary.

The limousine delivered them to the hotel where the event was taking place. She was helped out of the car, and Ramsey put his arm lightly around her shoulder. His touch made her pulse leap. She wasn't often nervous, but she was nervous now. Nervous because of the evening that lay ahead, more nervous because here she was, next to this handsome man exuding sexuality, his arm around her.

They were ushered into a palatial lobby where Samantha was relieved of her stole by a gray-haired man in a dark suit. Someone else escorted them into a large cocktail lounge where people in evening clothes were merrily mingling, drinks in hand.

And some crowd it was. Samantha stared, clamping her jaws together so as not to gape. Diamonds glittered, silk swirled, hair gleamed. She had no idea what important persons were there. She never read the society pages and she didn't move in art circles.

"How about a drink?" Ramsey said.

"Just some white wine, please."

He signaled a waiter who came rushing over and took Ramsey's order.

"MacMillan!" A man in an evening suit, movie-star handsome, strode toward them with outstretched hand. "Good to see you."

Ramsey introduced them, his voice businesslike. The man's name was Anthony Meecham, and he gave Samantha an appreciative look, smiling a gleaming set of teeth at her as he held her hand. "So, Samantha," he said, "what castle did you escape from?"

She was aware of Ramsey's wary expression as he watched the man look at her. She smiled. "It's white and red and very cozy."

"Excuse us, please," Ramsey said coolly, and led her away, in the direction of the waiter who was coming toward them with their drinks. And behind him, in shimmering silk, was Cecilia. Samantha groaned inwardly.

"Ramsey! How nice to see you!" Cecilia said, smiling a toothpaste smile. She put her hand possessively on Ramsey's arm. "How are you?"

"Fine, thank you," he said evenly. He turned to Samantha, drawing her closer against him. "Cecilia, you remember Samantha?"

The cold blue eyes narrowed slightly. "Yes, yes, although I didn't recognize you right away."

Of course not. When they'd met last week, Samantha had worn patched jeans and old sneakers.

Samantha steeled herself and forced a polite smile. "Hello, Cecilia."

The woman inclined her head and took a sip of her drink. "Hi," she said coolly, giving Samantha a frigid stare, then turning her attention back to Ramsey.

"I heard you were in Paris yesterday. Did you see Violet?"

Samantha felt the sudden tension in Ramsey's arm as it tightened around her.

"No," he said curtly. "Is Richard here?"

Cecilia waved her hand. "Somewhere over there. Oh, there's Julio. I must see him." She moved on, casting one more frosty look at Samantha.

Other people came up and claimed Ramsey's attention. He introduced her to all of them, men and women who smiled at her politely, questions in their eyes. She smiled, extended her hand, smiled some more, said the necessary pleasantries, hoping no one would ask her any difficult questions, all the while acutely aware of Ramsey's arm around her, the warmth of his body close to hers.

She listened to the people talk, hearing odds and ends of sentences and phrases.

"I know Taylor at the SEC. He owes me one."

"...fronted by the Dayaks and run by the Chinese."

"He had calf implants...skinny legs..."

At one point she realized she was no longer at Ramsey's side and for a moment panic hit her. Then she controlled herself. What could possibly happen to her?

All these glamorous people were just ordinary folks under all the finery. Happy and unhappy, nice and nasty, just like the rest of humanity, at least that was what her grandmother would say.

She stood still by a bank of huge potted palms and surveyed the room, sipping her drink. Voices and laughter all around. She didn't pay much attention until she heard someone mentioning Ramsey's name, a female voice floating through the palms from the other side of the grouping.

"Did you see his new woman?" the voice said. "Nobody knows who she is, isn't that strange? I mean, *nobody*. I asked around and they've never seen her before. I even asked Cassandra. If *she* doesn't know, who does?"

"Some reporter will come up with it," another invisible female said. "It'll be in the papers tomorrow."

"Maybe she's some senator's daughter."

"Somebody would know that."

"Right."

"What do you think? True love?"

"No way. She's after his money, just like the rest of us." Laughter silenced their voices for the next moment.

"By the way, what happened to Violet?"

"She's in Europe. I saw a picture of her with some Spanish count, or maybe Italian, I don't remember."

"What was her name again? I mean, Ramsey's new conquest? Samantha something?"

"Greene. Samantha Greene."

"I hate to say it, but she looks great. Walks like she's some royalty, and that dress is gorgeous."

"Suppose he ditched Violet?"

"Who knows? Maybe she ditched him."

"Not likely. Not our Violet. Unless she found somebody with more money."

"Or a title."

"*And* a title."

More laughter, then a martyred sigh. "Just the same, I wish I'd known he was *sans femme*. I wouldn't have minded comforting him."

"Neither would I. Let's have another drink and drown our sorrows."

The voices drifted away. Samantha realized she'd been holding her breath. Her heart was pounding. She inhaled slowly, then took a sip from her drink.

"You look rather lost," came a voice, and she glanced to the right to see a bearded face and a pair of intense blue eyes trained on her. "Or are you hiding from the blinding crowds?" The man was smiling at her, stroking his blond beard that matched the thick hair on top of his head.

She forced a smile. "It does rather glitter and sparkle around here, and no, I wasn't hiding. I'm merely observing."

He nodded. "An interesting pastime." He extended his hand. "I'm Jeremy Kramer."

"I'm Samantha Greene."

"You're with Ramsey MacMillan, right?"

"Yes." She took another sip from her drink. "I was looking for him, actually."

Jeremy waved his hand. "Over there, discussing a billion-dollar deal with Crawford. He won't miss you for the next few minutes."

She looked in the direction he had indicated. Ramsey's broad back was turned toward her and he was talking to two other men in evening clothes. She didn't know who Crawford was, although Jeremy Kramer seemed to think she did. Maybe everybody here did. Maybe, once you'd climbed your way into the rarefied atmosphere of high society, everybody knew everybody. It seemed so. Women were hugging each other and kissing the air next to carefully powdered cheeks. Men were slapping each other on the shoulder. It was like one big happy family, and she felt distinctly the outsider.

Thank heaven, she was dressed right. And thank you, Grandma, she said silently, for my ballet lessons.

"Do you think he'll pull it off?" Jeremy asked, his eyes on Ramsey and the two men.

Pull what off? She was supposed to know. "We can only wait and see," she said, sipping her drink.

"Crawford's a crafty bastard," said Jeremy.

"So I hear."

"Business, always business," he said. "Making money is like an addiction, you know. That's why it's never enough." He gave her a shrewd look.

She smiled. "So tell me, are you addicted to making money as well?"

He laughed. "Direct, are you?"

"It makes things simpler. Cuts down on confusion and misinterpretation."

He nodded. "Quite. And to answer your question, no, I'm not addicted to making money. I'm here merely to socialize. And to support the cause, of course," he added piously, his blue eyes glinting with humor.

"You like museums?"

"Never set a foot in them, actually, but someone bought me this ticket, so here I am. Tell me, are you a native Washingtonian, or an import?"

"Neither—I live in Virginia. And you?"

"Oh, I'm an import. I'm from Colorado, but I've lived here for the last ten years. So what do you do in Virginia, Samantha? Grow peanuts, tobacco?"

"Tomatoes, actually, in my backyard."

He grinned. "For a living?"

"For food. I'm a teacher, first grade."

"Is that so? How interesting."

"Is it? I was told it's quite a traditional profession for a woman, and very unfashionable these days."

"I don't meet many grade-school teachers."

She gestured around the room. "Not at these affairs, I imagine."

"Right."

He was easy to talk to. He was a food writer, he said, writing free-lance for papers and magazines. After a few more minutes, Samantha excused herself to join Ramsey,

who was still talking to the two men at the other side of
the room.

She didn't get far across the lounge. A woman stopped
her, taking her arm, not too gently.

"So, who are you?" she wanted to know.

Taken aback, Samantha stared at the woman. She
looked like a lizard in her skintight scaly dress. They'd
been introduced a while earlier, but Samantha couldn't
remember her name. Her pupils were huge and she
seemed none too steady on her high heels.

"I'm Samantha Greene."

"Yes, I know that. But who are you? What are your
connections? What the hell are you doing with Ramsey?"

"Oh, stop it, Leona! You're being obnoxious." The
friend in black velvet took her by the arm. She grimaced
apologetically at Samantha. "She's on a diet, and it
makes her cranky."

"I want to know who the hell she is!"

Samantha smiled, feeling the little devil inside her
coming out of hiding. "Actually, I don't know," she
said. "It's all a blank since the accident."

The two women stared at her.

"I have amnesia," Samantha offered helpfully. "All
I remember is waking up in Ramsey's bed. I had the
most ungodly headache." She sighed. "I couldn't remember how I got there, who he was, who I was…am."

The lizard woman's eyes nearly popped out. Samantha
smiled. "Please excuse me." She turned and walked out
of the room.

The air was cooler here. She took a deep breath and
willed her legs to stop shaking. Maybe she should just
stay here, hoping the vultures and barracudas wouldn't
notice her.

"What are you doing out here?" came Ramsey's voice.
She turned to face him.

"It feels safer out here," she said.

"Safer?"

"Not everyone is totally delighted to see me with you.
The moment you took off and left me to my own devices,

they came for me." She heard the anger in her voice and swallowed hard.

He frowned. "They came for you," he stated, as if he had suspected as much. "What did they say to you?"

"One grabbed me by the arm and demanded to know who I was. I heard somebody else suggesting I was a gold digger. I don't believe it's in the job description that I should take this kind of abuse from people." She took a deep breath. "And if it's part and parcel of this arrangement, let me tell you, you got yourself a bargain at eight grand!" She turned away and walked off, in the wrong direction.

Ramsey followed her, coming to stand beside her at a large window overlooking the city. "I'm sorry. I thought you'd be all right."

"Well, I wasn't. You seem to think that all I have to do is put on the appropriate clothing and I'll fit. Well, unfortunately it doesn't work that way." She clutched her evening bag, as if it could give her support. "This sort of thing is not my scene, as they say. I don't know a single soul in this entire room. I don't know what and who they're talking about. I'm out of my element and..." Her voice wobbled precariously. She bit her lip. "It's difficult," she said, trying to inject some dignity into her tone. She straightened her shoulders. "You can at least help me a little the first time. I'm a fast learner and it won't take me long, but don't just throw me in the water without teaching me a basic stroke!"

"All right, I won't leave you again. It simply didn't occur to me that this could be a problem, but we'll easily rectify it. Come along now, it's time to go in to dinner." He took her arm and led her back into the cocktail lounge and into the adjoining dining room along with the rest of the glittering crowd.

In the dining room all was silver and crystal and gleaming china. It was like a fairy tale, a fairy tale she'd tell her pupils, full of princes and princesses, precious jewels and chests full of treasures. And miracles. Of course there was always a miracle or two. But not in this fairy tale, because it was a fake one to start with. Fake fairy tales didn't deserve miracles.

They were seated at a large round table, and more introductions were made. Samantha was aware of the curious glances she received, of the attention Ramsey bestowed on her. He spoke to her privately, smiled at her, made sure she was doing all right.

A speaker appeared on a podium at the front of the room. Samantha listened to his presentation—profuse thanks for the support given to the project, the construction of a new museum. There was more, but she didn't really hear it. She was aware of Ramsey close to her, his dark eyes watching her. She kept thinking of Cecilia, and the woman who had demanded to know who she was. It wasn't a surprise to know there were women out there who had their eyes on Ramsey, but it would take talent and presence of mind to handle them.

The food was delicious. She managed to sit through the dinner, smiling a lot and saying little, which seemed perhaps the safest approach. With seven other people at the table, the conversation moved easily enough without her help. She listened, not understanding much, not being familiar with the topics or the people. Ramsey also was not a man of many words. She wondered if he enjoyed the evening or merely found it a big bore he needed to live through. It was hard to tell from his expression.

Fortunately, the meal progressed without further incident. Maybe she had overreacted. Maybe it was silly to get upset by what other people said or did.

Still, it was a relief to be back in the privacy of the limousine.

"What did you say when this woman demanded to know who you were?" Ramsey asked.

She bit her lip, suppressing a sudden smile.

"What's so funny?" he queried.

"I said something to her that was probably a mistake. It kind of slipped out." She could feel warmth creep into her cheeks.

He quirked a dark eyebrow. "And what was that?"

She gave him a pained expression. "You're not going to like it. I said that I didn't know who I was, because I suffered from amnesia and that one morning I—er..." She closed her eyes and groaned. "I don't know how to say this."

"Just say it."

She glanced away. "That one morning I woke up in—er—your bed and that I couldn't remember who I was or where I came from."

Silence. She didn't dare look at him. Then, to her surprise, she heard him laugh. He reached out and for a moment covered her hand with his.

"And you said you're worried about handling these people? You'll be fine. Better yet, you'll be great."

She hoped so.

The limo let them off in front of Ramsey's building. They stood together in the elevator. Samantha felt uneasy about what was to come, felt the apprehension creeping through her. Here she was with this man, this stranger, going up to his penthouse to stay the night.

"It's not even midnight," she said lightly, trying to cover up her nervousness. "I can change in five minutes and Simon can take me home. I won't mind."

"You've got nothing to worry about, Samantha," he assured her.

"I didn't say I was worried."

"But you are." His mouth curved slightly. "I'm in full command of my—er—baser instincts."

She felt heat rise to her cheeks, and looked away, fighting desperately for composure. He was in full command of everything. She, however, had lost her control and self-confidence. That was what happened when you weren't in your own element. Thinking of the weeks ahead, she felt panic rise.

The elevator stopped and moments later they were back in the apartment, the double doors closed and locked behind them. She felt as if she'd been locked away in a jail cell. Anything could happen here, and no one would know or notice.

Don't be an idiot, she said to herself. She glanced up at Ramsey. "I hope I didn't disappoint you. I'm afraid I wasn't worth much conversation-wise. I don't know much about what people were talking about."

"Half the time they don't know themselves either, and you were fine." He touched her hand. "It's just a big show."

"They raised a lot of money, show or no show." She bit her lip, and for a moment he looked at her silently.

"For a museum," he said quietly. "As if we don't have enough museums."

Her thoughts exactly, but she hadn't voiced them. Museums were important. Art was important—as a teacher she would never argue with that. Still, there were so many other needs and tragedies... "Why did you go?" she asked.

He shrugged. "It was expected. Both my parents were generous patrons of the arts. It's a family obligation, if you will."

And besides, what was a thousand dollars anyway? she thought. Peanuts for a man of his wealth.

"Would you care for another drink before going to... our separate beds?" he asked.

"Would you mind if I declined? I'm tired and I think I'd like to collapse and go to sleep."

"No, I don't mind." He searched her face. "Was it a terrible ordeal for you?"

"Actually, I learned a lot."

"Such as?"

"Well, let's see. Next time I'm in Kuala Lumpur, I'll know where to go for the most divine body massage. I know that the old King of Swaziland had over a hundred wives. And if you're into mycophagy you go nuts over eating wild mushrooms. It was very educational."

His mouth quirked. "It's comforting to know it wasn't a total waste of your time. Sleep well."

She wished him good-night and moved quickly down the hall to her bedroom. She closed the door behind her and almost kicked off her shoes, then thought better of it. Handmade Italian shoes deserved better treatment. She took them off carefully and arranged them in the cupboard. Then, with a deep sigh, she dropped herself down on the big bed.

"Mission accomplished," she said to the ceiling. "Number one, anyway."

She slept like the dead and didn't awake until after nine the next morning. She took a quick shower, dressed in black pants and a red sweater and left the bedroom. Faint noises came from the far direction of the hall. The living room was empty, but with further searching, she found the kitchen with Mrs. Gregory in it, chopping vegetables.

"Good morning, Mrs. Gregory."

The woman looked up in surprise. "Good morning. I didn't hear you. Did you sleep well?"

"Yes, thank you."

Mrs. Gregory moved into action, pouring coffee and heating some croissants, which Samantha ate in the kitchen, rather than the breakfast room, as Mrs. Gregory suggested.

"Where's Mr. MacMillan?" Samantha asked.

"He left early this morning. He's in New York for the day. He left this for you." Mrs. Gregory handed her a sealed envelope.

"Thank you." Samantha put it aside. She'd look at it later.

After breakfast she went back into her room to get her things. She slit the envelope open and extracted a sheet of paper. It was a calendar of events for the month of December—more benefits, a gallery opening, dinners, a cocktail party at the Argentine Embassy, a reception for a visiting Japanese diplomat. She perused the list with a growing apprehension. After each event was a short description, and the clothing required. A note scrawled across the top stated that a credit card was forthcoming.

She had not expected to be out with Ramsey so many nights in just a few weeks. She had not expected him to spend such staggering amounts of money on her.

She felt suddenly filled with a sense of the absurd, and she began to laugh. This was the craziest thing that had ever happened to her. But then rich people were known to do the most bizarre and unbelievable things, like having swimming pools lined with gold, or keeping Bengal tigers for pets.

Compared to that, Ramsey buying her clothes was nothing. She might as well enjoy it while it lasted.

The limousine took her back home. The house seemed suddenly very small, but she didn't mind. It was a warm and friendly house, and it was hers.

Melissa phoned that afternoon, breathless with curiosity. "Tell me all," she demanded. "I wish I could come over, but it's my grandmother's birthday and we're having the whole family at my parents' for dinner and I'm helping out."

Samantha told all, rather dramatizing the story of the lizard woman. By the time she was finished, they were both weak with laughter.

"I wish I could have been there," said Melissa.

"I could have used the support. I don't like feeling intimidated."

"You rallied to the challenge. So when is your next event? Oh, sorry, somebody's calling me. I'd better go. I'll call you later."

Monday went by like any other Monday, filled with children and teaching and taking care of her responsibilities for ACTION. At times Samantha wondered if Saturday night had been merely a fantasy, a figment of her overactive imagination. But Ramsey's schedule of events taped to her refrigerator door would bring everything back into clear focus.

She was cooking dinner when Ramsey called. "I'm at the airport. Can I drop by for a moment?"

"Yes, of course."

"I'll be right there."

She put the phone down with a trembling hand. Her heart was racing. This was crazy! What was the matter with her? She ran into the bathroom and looked at herself. Her eyes were glittering oddly. Her hair was a mess. She brushed it out and put on some lipstick, then glanced at her clothes. She wore a short, slim skirt, a big colorful sweater and color-coordinated stockings. This was the real her, and it had to be good enough.

She went back into the kitchen and chopped up some parsley and added it to the soup.

Fifteen minutes later the limousine drew up to the house. From the living room window she watched as Simon held the door open and Ramsey emerged into the yellow glow of the porch light. She willed herself to be calm as she went to open the door to let him in.

"Hi," she said, and he smiled down at her, returning the greeting.

"Is this an inconvenient time?" he asked.

"No. I was just cooking myself some soup."

"Not canned, I hope," he said, as he entered the room.

"Oh, no. It's genuine homemade root soup."

"Root soup? Sounds..."

"I know," she said, nodding, feeling laughter tickling her throat.

"What is it?"

"Soup made of roots—potatoes, carrots, onions, turnips, whatever. There's no particular recipe. You cook it in chicken broth, add celery and parsley, or whatever, and milk. Some ham if you have it, and salt and pepper, of course."

"Very scientific."

She gave him a solemn look. "It takes great creativity to do it right."

"I can imagine."

"It's delicious, and very nutritious. You're just spoiled, eating caviar every day."

His mouth quirked. "Heaven forbid!"

"Why don't you try it?" she said boldly, surprised to hear the words come out. "You took me to dinner last Saturday, so let me reciprocate." It was the little devil inside her talking, no doubt about that. She bit her lip and gave him a challenging look.

He didn't miss the challenge in her eyes and for a moment he held her gaze, then he slightly inclined his head. "Thank you, I'd like that."

"Really?" She laughed. "That's great. I didn't think you'd accept."

"Why wouldn't I?"

"Well, let's see. One: you're too busy. Two: root soup sounds disgusting. Three: you have a meeting somewhere. Four: you have work to do, et cetera, et cetera."

"Nonetheless, a man has to eat sometimes."

She nodded. "I'm of the same opinion." She made to turn away. "Let me set the table."

Ramsey touched her shoulder. "Wait just a minute." He fished something out of the inner breast pocket of his jacket and handed it to her. "This should facilitate your shopping excursions."

It was a credit card. Gold and shiny, even the piece of plastic looked expensive.

"Wow!" she said, injecting a proper amount of awe into her voice. "I could buy myself diamonds with this. Or a BMW."

"Somehow I don't think that's your style," he said dryly. "You seem to be more interested in putting roofs over people's heads and keeping food on their tables."

She gave a light shrug. "Oh, well, a girl has to do something to keep busy if she doesn't have a card like this."

"Alicia told me she's going to help you buy clothes."

"Right." She grinned. "Should be quite an adventure—Cinderella getting decked out for the ball."

He raised a dark brow. "You're no Cinderella."

"Why not?"

He smiled now. "You're a teacher. Don't you know your fairy tales? Cinderella was a helpless victim, abused by a trio of mean women. You, dear Samantha, are about as independent and together as anyone I know, ball gown or no ball gown."

She gave an exaggerated sigh. "Oh, heck, I kind of liked the Cinderella idea. Well, let me get the soup on the table. Have a seat." She leaned over and whipped her knitting out of the chair by the fire. It was a sleeve for a sweater she was making as a Christmas present for Paul.

Ramsey glanced at the knitting in her hand, then back at her. "Don't tell me you knit too."

"Is that strange?"

"I thought only little old ladies knitted these days."

"My grandmother was a little old lady, and she taught me." Samantha made a prim and proper face. "I had a very old-fashioned upbringing—sort of. It's a cross I have to bear." She turned away. "We can eat in just a minute."

In the kitchen she tasted the soup. It was delicious, parsnips and all, but she must be out of her mind to ask him to stay. He didn't belong here in this cozy little kitchen with his three-piece suit. It was so strange to see all this sophistication amid the bright clutter of her small house.

Maybe that was exactly why she'd asked him. Because it appealed to her sense of the ridiculous. Because she wanted to see if he'd accept. And he had, so now she'd better feed him.

After she'd quickly set the table with bowls and plates for bread, she called him in. "You can take off your jacket if you like," she offered. "I don't stand on formality in this house."

"I'm quite comfortable, thank you." His eyes held humor, as if he knew very well what it was she was doing. Well, of course he knew. If he were stupid he wouldn't be driving around in a limousine running a multibillion-dollar company.

He ate with appetite. "It's good," he said after a few spoonfuls. "Did your grandmother teach you to cook too?"

Samantha nodded. "Yes, but this soup is my own invention."

"Tell me about that old-fashioned upbringing of yours."

"My grandparents raised me, here in this house." She shrugged. "We never had much money, but it never seemed we needed anything. We had everything. My grandmother had a big garden and she put up lots of food for the winter, and my grandfather hunted deer. I went hunting with him once, but I couldn't shoot. I came face-to-face with a deer and it looked at me with those big brown eyes and I just couldn't do it. After that I never went with him again. I stuck to cooking and knitting and ballet." She grinned. "Girl stuff, but it's what I liked."

"Why did your grandparents bring you up? No, don't answer that. I'm being indiscreet."

She laughed. "I don't mind answering." He was curious and for a moment his control had lapsed. It was an interesting thought. She wiped her mouth with her napkin. "My parents drowned in a boating accident when I was only four months old. I know it sounds awful, and it was, of course, but I never knew them. I have no memory of them, but I had a family. To all intents and purposes my grandparents were my parents, and Paul was my brother, although really he's my uncle. He's only twelve years older than I am, my grandparents' late-life surprise, so to speak. I had a very happy, normal childhood, so please don't feel sorry for me."

Ramsey nodded. "It's a deal."

She ladled more soup on her spoon. "What about your parents?" she asked.

"Divorced when I was eight. My mother lives in Hawaii. My father died of a heart attack six years ago.

I have no brothers or sisters." He enumerated the facts as if they were information on an application form, his face expressionless.

It was the only personal information he apparently was prepared to part with, although she found out that he often made business trips overseas and played tennis— hence the tan. He consumed two bowls of soup, while she tried to draw him out, without much success. He fielded every question craftily and turned the conversation right back to her. Obviously he was more interested in hearing about her than in talking about himself. So she kept the conversation going, watching him while he ate, looking at his face, his eyes, his hands, wondering what lay behind the cool, sophisticated facade. Wondering what it would feel like to be touched by those hands.

She felt a growing curiosity, a growing need to know, and she wondered why. Was it simply because it was difficult for her to pass up a challenge? Or was it something else?

Ramsey stood up to leave soon after the meal was over. "Thank you," he said, hand on the doorknob. "I enjoyed that."

"So did I." She leaned her back against the wall, sensing in him a certain reluctance to leave despite the hand on the doorknob. He didn't move, and the silence began to quiver with an awkward tension. His dark eyes probed hers and she felt her stomach flutter uneasily. Why was he looking at her like that? What was it that he was thinking and not saying? She tried to say something to break the silence, some clever remark that would make him smile, but no thoughts, no words presented themselves.

She couldn't move, couldn't tear her eyes away.

"It's just as well you're not Cinderella," he said softly. He paused for a fraction of a moment, his eyes still holding hers captive. "I'm no prince, Samantha."

CHAPTER FIVE

THE rest of the week went by in a dizzy dance of activity—teaching, shopping for clothes, attending a cocktail party with Ramsey on Friday night.

Samantha had explained the situation to both Melissa and Alicia and sworn them to secrecy. Alicia had said she would be delighted to help Samantha with her wardrobe. As a matter of fact, buying clothes was one of her favorite pastimes.

Both Alicia and Melissa had offered to take over some of Samantha's work and responsibilities with ACTION, much to her relief.

"It's all for the good of the cause," Melissa said in a long-suffering voice. "You play the princess and we'll do the work."

"If you think all this is so great, you should try dealing with those women who are after Ramsey. They're vicious," Samantha told her.

Melissa shrugged. "Give me a gorgeous gown, a guy like Ramsey on my arm, and I can handle anybody." She paused. "And so can you."

Samantha made a face. "Let's say I'm learning."

She was learning more than she had ever wanted to know about expensive clothes, designers, fabrics, styles. She was grateful for Alicia's help. She was also grateful for the information on Ramsey that Alicia imparted. Alicia talked easily and much prompting wasn't necessary.

"I don't think he trusts a lot of people," she'd said while they were out shopping for clothes. "It's hard when you know everybody wants something from you—information, influence, favors, money, a good deal. I think he never married because of that. His experiences with

women may not have been very positive, but I'm
guessing. Oh, look at this color, isn't it lovely?'' She
reached out to a wine-colored gown the saleslady was
holding up for their inspection.

"It is. I'm not sure about the neckline, though."

"Try it on. You might be surprised."

Samantha took the gown into the sumptuous dressing
room. They'd selected three dresses already.

Alicia sat down on a stool and crossed her slim legs.
"Ramsey was a lot more fun when we were kids. They
own a villa on Saint Barlow, in the Caribbean, and we
used to go on vacation there. It was great. We'd go sailing
and swimming and snorkeling. He wasn't nearly as
serious then. I think his parents' divorce really affected
him. I liked my uncle, but Ramsey's mother is a witch,
but don't tell him I said that. Do you need me to help
you zip it up?"

"Please."

Alicia got up from the stool and carefully zipped up
the dress. "There's an orphanage on Saint Barlow. Some
of the kids are in bad shape and they come to
Philadelphia for medical treatment. Friends of Ramsey's
are involved in it and he spends tons of money paying
the medical bills." She stepped in front of Samantha
and grinned. "There's a soft heart somewhere under all
that cool composure. Amazing, isn't it?" She stepped
back and studied Samantha critically. "It's wonderful,
really. That color is very exotic."

And so it went. From Alicia's casual remarks, tossed
in between fittings and quick cups of coffee, a picture
formed in Samantha's mind. Ramsey, running the family-
owned corporation, making work his life, jetting back
and forth between continents. He owned a villa in the
south of France, an apartment in Hong Kong, other
apartments in London and Paris. Apart from work-
related activities, not much else seemed to fill his life.
Not even the women seemed to play a major part,
existing on the fringes only.

"He's so damned self-contained," Alicia said one day. "At least, that's what you'd think. But it's not natural, you know. Everybody *needs* to be connected to other people. Don't you agree?"

"So what's wrong with him? Why is he that way?"

Alicia shook her sleek auburn head. "I don't know. Maybe he really doesn't expect to ever be loved. Maybe he doesn't believe in love."

Saturday afternoon, coming home from another shopping spree, Samantha found an unfamiliar car in her driveway. As she approached, the door opened and a man got out.

She remembered his face, the blond beard—the man she had spoken to at the party at some length. She searched her memory for his name.

"Jeremy Kramer, remember?" he asked.

She smiled. "Oh, yes, I remember. How did you know where to find me?" She hadn't told him where she lived, what small town in Virginia.

He laughed. "It wasn't hard. You're a grade-school teacher. That's enough to go by for a creative person with a few connections."

"So, to what do I owe this honor?" she asked lightly.

He shrugged. "I was in Leesburg this afternoon, so I thought I'd stop by on the off chance that you'd be free for dinner."

"I'm afraid I'm not, but thank you for asking. I'm going into town tonight."

"With MacMillan?"

"Yes." She put her key in the lock. "I hope you'll excuse me," she said, "but I'm running late."

"No problem. See you around, Samantha." He climbed back into his car, started the engine, waved through the window and was gone.

To her surprise, she saw him again that evening. He was talking to an African in flowing robes, and he smiled at her and waved his hand, but did not approach her all evening. Was it a coincidence that he was there at the same place? She shrugged the thought away, and tried to concentrate on the conversation around her.

There was talk of futures and currencies, of the eating habits of a South American potentate, of killer bees invading the country, of economics and politics.

"What do you think, Samantha?" someone asked politely. She was probably making the man uncomfortable with her silence. Possibly her smile had taken on a certain aura of senility after being fixed on her face for so long—it was hard to tell; there was no mirror in her immediate vicinity.

What did she think? About what? She tried to relax her mouth.

"I believe that many strategies are shortsighted," she said bravely. She had read that phrase in the paper this morning. "We should act with long-term goals in mind, but, of course, we Americans aren't very good at postponing gratification. We all love our instant oatmeal, don't we?" She smiled again.

"I love apple cinnamon flavor," said a plump woman in purple sequins.

Samantha swallowed, faked a cough to cover up the violent impulse to laugh. She coughed again.

Ramsey drew her away. "Let's get you a drink. Excuse us," he said to the others, and led her away.

"I don't need a drink," she said, taking a deep breath.

"I know." There was a glint of humor in his eyes. "I needed an excuse to get away from that group of brilliant intellectuals."

By the time they left, about an hour later, Samantha was beginning to think she'd not get her face to relax again. She'd be cursed with a perpetual smile.

"Was all this a big bore?" Ramsey asked when Simon had driven them back to the penthouse.

After being on her feet for several hours, she was glad to be sitting down. "Oh, no, I like watching people, wondering what they're really like, what they're thinking."

"What do you think they're thinking?"

"Well, most of them aren't there for fun, that's obvious, although they're all pretending to have a wonderful time. It seems to me they're all out hunting for something or other, sizing each other up to see if they can be useful in some way or other. Networking, I believe it's called. People don't like each other for what they are, only for what they can get out of them. That's a pretty sorry state of affairs, if you ask me."

"That's the way the game is played."

"A game. That's all it is?"

"Of course. The game of life, at least here."

"Power and wealth. And I look at all that wealth, all that money...it's...overwhelming. This afternoon, right before Simon picked me up, I was putting together two food deliveries, and now I'm here, eating smoked salmon. It makes me feel schizophrenic."

He smiled. "You'll get used to it."

They arrived at the apartment and went up in the elevator, standing close in the small space, not touching. Samantha felt again the strange tension between them, noticed how he seemed more formal when he spoke to her, as if somehow the intimacy of the small space was a strain. When they were together in public he would put his arm around her or hold her hand, claiming her for his own for the world to see. But when they were alone in the limousine or elevator he never held her hand, never touched her.

Once inside his apartment, he wished her good-night and Samantha took herself to the beautiful room that was hers to use, and went to bed.

Again she dreamed of him. She was always dreaming of him.

"Sam, you're falling for him," Melissa said one day, having dropped by for a cup of coffee after finishing work at the hospital. "It's dangerous, don't you know that?"

"Don't be ridiculous!" Samantha spooned sugar into her coffee and stirred it a little too vigorously. Coffee sloshed over the edge of the cup.

"All you ever do is talk about him."

Samantha shrugged. "Of course I do. It's all very exciting—all these clothes, the people, the parties, the food. It's *unreal*. Of course I talk about it all the time." She got up from the table and opened the doors to the wood stove and prodded the logs. "It's cold in here, isn't it?"

"No, it isn't, and you're changing the subject." Melissa sighed. "Sam, you know I'm right. It's in your eyes and in your voice, in everything you say."

Samantha straightened and sat down again. "Melissa, you may not believe this, but he's *nice*. I like him. He's an intriguing man."

"He's handsome and he's rich, I'll give you that. He's also a businessman, and he's ruthless and sharp and arrogant. He's using you, Sam."

"That's not true. We have an agreement."

"Oh, don't give me that, Sam!"

"Well, it's true. Eight thousand dollars isn't a present."

"All right, you have an agreement. And you're in love with him. It's a recipe for disaster, Sam! You're going to get hurt!"

Samantha said nothing. It wasn't any use denying her feelings. Melissa knew her too well.

"Sam, what can this possibly lead to?" Melissa persisted.

Samantha bit her lip. "Nothing, I suppose." A wealthy, sophisticated man like Ramsey MacMillan wasn't going to get seriously involved with a girl like her. And it had been clear from the beginning. He had never lied to her. He had never tried to take advantage of her. "It's just as well you're not Cinderella," he'd said. "I'm no prince." It had been a warning and she knew it. But warnings didn't do much to deter instinctive feelings. Warnings were for the mind, not for the heart.

Yet he liked her—she was sure about that. He seemed to enjoy her company, enjoy listening to her. By now, he knew a lot about her. He encouraged her to talk about herself, and she didn't mind. What she did mind was that he revealed so very little about himself. She was minding it more and more.

Yesterday she'd noticed him observing her again with that dark, brooding look in his eyes. She caught him often doing that, and it made her uneasy.

"I feel like you're always looking at me, observing me," she'd said. "You make me talk about myself, but you won't talk about yourself."

"It isn't part of the agreement."

"Oh, right. Sorry." She'd felt hurt, and it had made her angry with herself. There was no reason to feel hurt. They weren't working on a relationship, and she should never forget that. She was merely doing a job—a temporary job, at that. To all intents and purposes, he was her boss, and he was the one calling the shots. And in a few weeks it would all be over.

It was stupid to fall in love with him. It wouldn't lead anywhere. She'd get hurt, like Melissa said.

She drank from her coffee and looked at Melissa. "I suppose I'll get over it," she said.

She finished Paul's sweater that night, and it was gorgeous, easy competition to the expensive hand-knitted sweaters she'd seen in the stores. The Italian design was beautiful and the color combination had worked very well. She held it up and admired it, and a thought crept unbidden into her mind.

This would look great on Ramsey.

Rasmey in a sweater. She'd never seen him in anything more casual than a navy blazer and tan pants. He was always working or going out to some flashy event, either in a dark three-piece suit or evening clothes.

If she started knitting now, and really pushed, she might just be able to finish a sweater for Ramsey before Christmas.

She could give it to him for Christmas.

Maybe it was inappropriate, too personal a present for a business relationship. Samantha bit her lip. But it was the only thing she could do that would be real. He didn't need one more business gift—cans of caviar, or expensive wine or gift baskets with French pâtés with truffles or whatever.

Was it really so crazy to give him something? He'd taken her out to so many places, had been so nice to her.

Nice. She closed her eyes briefly, pushing down the sudden wave of longing. If only there were a little more than nice. Sometimes she imagined there was something more than nice, something more than casual interest in the way he looked and smiled at her, the way he touched her, held her hand. But it couldn't be—it was all for show, to keep away the vultures. Thinking there was more than that was just wishful dreaming, the product of an overactive imagination.

She shouldn't hope for the impossible, shouldn't allow herself to long for what she couldn't have.

She took the sweater, folded it carefully and packed it in a box lined with red tissue paper. She could knit Ramsey a sweater and decide later if she should give it to him or not. If she decided not to, there'd be no problem getting rid of it. People were always asking her to knit sweaters for them. There was a boutique owner who'd asked more than once to buy her creations, only she never had time. What she liked even better than knitting sweaters was teaching six-year-olds.

The next afternoon Samantha was barely home from school when Lee Ann called. Her voice sounded odd, and Samantha felt an immediate sense of alarm.

"What's wrong, Lee Ann?" she demanded urgently.

"Everything. Murphy's Law, isn't that what it's called? Everything that can go wrong, will go wrong. Well, everything did. Mrs. Grand left a few days ago to be with her daughter in Florida who's just had a baby.

The next day the girls got the chickenpox, both of them, and..." Lee Ann took a deep breath. "You'll never believe this, Sam, but I just broke my leg!"

"Oh, good Lord, Lee Ann, how did you do that?"

A long story followed, about how Lee Ann had tripped and fallen down the stairs, how Paul was in New York, working, and wouldn't be back until Sunday night, how one friend had stayed with the girls, and another had gone to the hospital with her.

"Where's Paul now?" asked Samantha. "Didn't he come home?"

"He doesn't know yet—I didn't want them to call him. This case is so important, Sam, and I'm not dying, after all, and neither are the girls, although we all feel like we are."

Samantha had heard about the case. If all went well, no doubt Paul would be offered a partnership, but he was paying dearly for it, working long hours and even weekends like this one, away from home.

"How are you feeling?" she asked.

"It hurts. I can't walk, and the girls are going crazy itching. You should see them. They look like something out of a horror movie, plastered in calamine lotion, and all these bumps all over them. The older you are, the worse it is, you know, and they're already twelve. They can't sleep because of the itching. Kirsten was practically hysterical last night, and I called the doctor and he finally gave us something to make both of them sleep." Lee Ann's voice wobbled. "Oh, Sam, I hate to ask, but could you possibly come over here for a couple of days to help out? I called my mother, but she can't get a flight until Sunday, with all the flights being booked for Christmas travel, and I don't know what else to do, with Mrs. Grand gone and Paul not here."

"Oh, Lee Ann, of course I'll come! I'll get packed and get started right away. I'll be there tonight." Thank goodness, the roads were clear and there was no snow in the forecast. Samantha ran into the bedroom, then suddenly froze as a thought occurred to her.

She was supposed to be getting ready for a reception for a visiting dignitary from Japan. It had completely escaped from her thoughts as she'd heard about Lee Ann's plight.

She couldn't just pack up and leave.

Her heart began to race. Oh, no, she couldn't get out of that. Ramsey was counting on her. The limo would be here for her in a couple of hours.

Panic rose to her head. She'd have to call Lee Ann... No, no, she couldn't let her down. She and Paul were the only family she had, and they'd always been there for her. Now they needed her. She couldn't let them down, not with Paul working on his case and Lee Ann and the children sick and the housekeeper out of state and no one else to help out.

What about her agreement with Ramsey?

Well, he'd just have to understand. Family came first. It had to come first. She took a deep breath, clenching her hands into fists as if ready to fight.

What if he didn't understand? She had a business agreement with him. If she didn't fulfill her part, he wouldn't have to fulfill his. ACTION needed the money. It wasn't as if it was hers. It was for food and housing for people who were hungry and cold, for children who lived in unheated houses. They needed the money... She couldn't take the risk of losing it.

She reached for the phone. She'd call him, try to explain. Surely he would understand?

The secretary said he was in a meeting and could not be disturbed.

Samantha took a deep breath. "It's an emergency," she said. "I must speak with him now."

She could almost feel the hesitation vibrate across the line.

"I really don't think—"

"One minute is all I need."

"Can't you give me a message?"

"No," she said bravely, praying.

"Oh, wait! You're in luck—they're just coming out. Just a moment."

Silence on the line. Samantha bit her lip, aware she was nervous, her heart beating erratically.

"MacMillan here," came Ramsey's voice, short, clipped, impatient.

"Ramsey—" she swallowed hard "—I'm terribly sorry to disturb you, but I have a huge problem. I can't make it tonight. I..."

"Yes, you can. We have an agreement. If you have a problem—"

"I do! I..."

"Are you ill? Kidnapped?"

"No!"

"In that case, whatever the problem is, manage it, make arrangements, delegate, whatever it takes. I need you."

She felt her heart sink. *I need you*, he said. Words that weren't meant the way she would have liked. The way he meant them, she didn't want to hear them. It left a bitter taste in her mouth. It also, somehow, made her furious.

"Ramsey, listen to me!" she begged.

"I have no time." His voice was cool and peremptory. "We've discussed this before, and I have no inclination to go over the same thing twice. Make your arrangements and I'll see you tonight."

The line went dead.

She slammed the receiver down. Damn him! Mr. High and Mighty! Too busy to talk to her, too important to concern himself with her problems. To hell with him. She was inclined, right then and there, to call the whole deal off, but of course she could not. She could not let her pride get in the way of the much-needed money.

She sank down on the bed, her mind going around in frantic circles. Lee Ann needed her. ACTION needed the money. Lee Ann needed her. ACTION needed the money.

There had to be a solution.

She stared unseeingly out the window at the bleak winter landscape.

She couldn't think of anything.

What was she going to do?

CHAPTER SIX

"MELISSA, what am I supposed to do?" Samantha wailed, running her hands through her hair in a gesture of despair.

At Samantha's panicked call for aid, Melissa had rushed over, not even bothering to change out of her nurse's uniform. She frowned darkly into a cup of hot coffee, as if an answer might be hiding in the murky depths of the brew.

"You can hardly say to the only family you have, 'Sorry, I've got to go to a party.' I'd go to Philadelphia for you, but I'm doing the three-to-eleven shift tomorrow."

"So what am I going to do? I made a deal with him, and we can't afford to let that money go. We *need* that money."

Melissa frowned. "Don't you think he'll understand?"

Samantha grimaced. "I called him, but he wouldn't even listen! He told me in no uncertain terms to make arrangements, delegate, organize. He's fully expecting me to be there tonight."

"That just isn't reasonable, Sam!"

"You tell him that! He's a businessman, after all," she said bitterly. "A deal is a deal."

"Did you tell him why you couldn't?"

"I didn't get a chance! He didn't care enough to ask!" She waved her hand in a frustrated gesture.

"The bastard!" Melissa said with feeling.

Samantha took a drink from her coffee. "Well, I suppose he didn't get to be so successful by being soft and sentimental. He wants a woman with him, and he's paying for it. Why should he pay if he doesn't get what he wants?"

A woman. The word echoed in her head. Maybe it didn't need to be her. She was just the one he found handy. She stared at Melissa, her heart racing again with sudden hope.

"Melissa, you go with him!"

Melissa's eyes grew wide. "You've got to be kidding," she said on a low note. "I can't do that!"

"Why not? If I can, you can."

Melissa jumped up and waved her hands. "I haven't got any clothes."

Samantha jumped up too. "You can wear the dress we bought for it—the blue one you liked so much! You even tried it on! Come on." She dragged Melissa into her bedroom. Opening the cupboard, she carefully took out the long cobalt blue gown and draped it on the bed. She'd taken it out of its protective bag the night before and had laid out everything else she would need—shoes, jewelry, her wrap. She gave Melissa a pleading look. "Please!"

Melissa shook her head. "I don't even know the man! He doesn't know me!"

"You met him—besides, it doesn't matter! It's just a job." Samantha said the words automatically, yet they hurt to say. They hurt all the way deep down inside. "All he wants is an arm piece," she added for good measure. She heard the bitterness in her own voice.

"An arm piece?"

"Some female on your arm who looks good and smiles nicely. Somebody to keep the vultures away. You'd be great for the job."

Melissa rolled her eyes. "Gee, you make me feel so good, so valued."

"Melissa, please! Remember, you envied me! This is your chance! You can see for yourself what it's like to mix with the movers and the shakers. Here's your chance to play the princess."

Melissa swallowed, hesitation in her eyes. "What's Ramsey going to say?" she asked.

"I don't think he cares as long as he has some presentable female on his arm—and for heaven's sake don't get offended. We're not doing this for love or ego. We're doing it for money."

"It sounds sleazy."

"There's nothing sleazy about that limousine or those parties or the food. And there's absolutely nothing sleazy about Ramsey. He's the perfect gentleman."

Oh, was he ever.

Melissa bit her lip and said nothing.

"I'll call right now. Please, say yes. It's not for me, it's for ACTION. Think of what we can do with the money! Please, Melissa!"

Several pleases later, Melissa succumbed, looking longingly at the blue dress.

Samantha called Ramsey's office, only to be told he was not in and was not expected back in his office. She felt a terrible sense of doom.

"I can't get hold of him," she said dully. She looked at her watch. "The limo will be here at seven."

"With him in it?"

"Probably not. Usually just Simon, the driver, picks me up and then I change at Ramsey's apartment, but, as luck will have it, not today. I was supposed to get ready at home and the limo was going to take me straight to the party."

"I can't go if Ramsey doesn't know about it!" Melissa's voice held terror.

"I'll let him know. You can get ready here. Get your mom to come and help you. I'll go on my way and I'll stop by the road somewhere in an hour or so and call him, or leave him a message, or something. I promise he'll know before you see him. I'll call Simon on the car phone. Let me try if I can find him."

Samantha dialed the limo number and Simon answered.

"Simon, this is Samantha. I have an urgent message for Mr. MacMillan, but I can't get hold of him just now. Will you see him before you leave to come here?"

"Yes, I will. Would you like me to give him a message?"

"Yes—I mean, tell him I'll be calling him on this line. What would be a good time?"

"About five-fifteen."

"Oh, thank you!" She replaced the receiver.

Ten minutes later she was packed and on the road. She tried to relax behind the wheel. There was nothing she could do now until five-fifteen when she had to call Ramsey. She kept glancing at her watch, checking the time. At five she started looking for a rest stop or a gas station. At five-thirteen she found one, and pulled off the road.

With trembling fingers she dialed the number of the limo, and Ramsey picked up the phone on the first ring.

She took a deep breath and leaned against the glass wall of the booth. "Ramsey, it's Samantha. I solved the problem."

"Good. What's all that noise I'm hearing?"

"Traffic. A semi just rolled by. I'm at a gas station. I'm on my way to Philadelphia and—"

"I believe you're supposed to be with me tonight." The voice, cold and sharp, cut through the distance.

"I know, I know, but I found you somebody else. My friend Melissa will—"

"You *what*?"

She gripped the receiver hard, willing herself to stay calm. "Melissa will come with you. She's great at keeping vultures at bay. She's got a stare that kills." Remembering how she'd left Melissa, nervous and apprehensive, she almost giggled. "She's at my house getting ready. It's no problem, honestly."

"This is not the agreement we had," he said coldly.

She felt a shiver go down her spine. "I know, I know. I'm terribly sorry, but I've got to go help Lee Ann and the girls. They need me. I have no choice, and Melissa was willing to do it, but it wasn't easy to convince her."

"Is that right?" The sarcasm in his voice was hard to miss.

"Yes. Oh, please, don't take this the wrong way. I mean..." Samantha glanced out of the window. Somebody was waiting to use the phone, a huge man in oily coveralls and a black, bushy beard. He glared at her impatiently. "Don't worry about it, she's great. You met her, remember? She's blond and gorgeous and—"

"Spare me the details. This will not do, Samantha. I want you—that's the agreement we had."

"I can't help it! I'm sorry! You told me to handle it and I did. I tried to do my best!"

She was interrupted by an angry tap on the glass. "Listen, I've got to go. Attila the Hun is waiting to use the phone. Please don't be mad."

"We'll discuss this later." Ramsey hung up and she made a face at the receiver, then quickly called her own number, giving the man a pleading look though the glass. Melissa answered.

"It's me, Samantha. I just talked to Ramsey, and he knows. How are you doing?"

"I just got out of the shower. Mom's coming over in a few minutes. She thinks this is great." Melissa sounded if she doubted her mother's sanity.

"An opportunity of a lifetime. Who knows? Maybe you'll meet your future husband tonight, a rich one. I've got to go, somebody's waiting to use the phone. He's about three hundred pounds and looks like an unhappy gorilla. 'Bye, good luck!"

Samantha felt bad about having to cut the conversation short, but she was afraid the man waiting out in the cold would have bodily dragged her out in another minute.

She vacated the phone booth, giving the man a dazzling smile. "My apologies," she said with as much charm as she could muster.

He stared at her with his mouth half-open, no doubt in readiness for some rude comment. Apparently her smile and the civil comment was not what he had expected and left him disarmed. Samantha grinned as she walked away.

All during the long dark drive, her thoughts kept coming back to Ramsey, wondering and worrying. She kept hearing his angry voice.

We'll talk later, he'd said. What if he decided not to continue the agreement? What if... what if...?

She wasn't looking forward to the discussion.

She found the household in a state of misery and turmoil when she arrived. One of the girls opened the door, looking like a chalky pink nightmare. The other one appeared at the top of the stairs and promptly broke out in tears. With the goop smeared all over their arms and faces, Samantha couldn't even tell them apart. Lee Ann lay on the sofa, glassy-eyed. "I don't know what's in this medicine," she wailed. "I'm seeing things! There are witches crawling all over the walls! What did they give me, Samantha?"

Samantha looked at the three of them, registering their expressions of hope and relief at her being there. Somebody had better take charge.

With that, she pushed Ramsey determinedly out of her mind.

Well, she tried.

Melissa called on Saturday morning. "How is everybody?" she asked.

"Miserable, but surviving." The night had been a trial. The girls had awakened several times, crazy with itching. Samantha felt bleary-eyed with lack of sleep. "How about you?"

"Well, I made it back untouched and unmolested." Melissa chuckled. "He *is* a gentleman, Sam! Perfectly polite and all that, and so very controlled. Quite intimidating, actually."

"So how did you like mingling with the rich and powerful?"

Melissa laughed. "It was an educational experience."

*   *   *

Rain slashed against the car windows with a force that rendered the windshield wipers helpless. Hunched over the steering wheel, her body rigid, Samantha peered through the wall of rain, trying not to lose track of the road. She tried to follow the red taillights of the car in front of her, praying the driver could see where he was going.

It was Sunday, and Lee Ann's mother had arrived late in the morning and Samantha had taken off as soon as possible after that, hoping the forecast winter storm would stay west and not hit until she was safely back in Aurora. It hadn't.

If there hadn't been the dinner to attend with Ramsey tonight, she would not have left. Now she wished she hadn't. No amount of money was worth risking your life for. "Oh, damn you, Ramsey," she muttered, "it's all your fault."

After a while the rain eased up and she could see the damage done by water and wind all around her. Cars run off the road, trees torn out of the ground. In front of her, under a leaden, threatening sky, the road stretched out into eternity. The wind was tearing at her little car, but there was no place to stop, so she kept on going. When the rain started up again, she clenched her jaw and prayed.

The road stretched. The hours stretched. Her nerves stretched. How she made it home, she didn't know. Exhaustion dulled her senses. She didn't even bother to bring her overnight bag into the house. All she wanted was to be inside and feel the safety of her own house surrounding her like a warm blanket. The tension finally relieved, she stood in the living room, shaking from reaction.

With trembling hands, she started a fire in the stove, then went into the kitchen and made a cup of hot chocolate. She sat on the couch, feet up, sipping it, feeling the soothing warmth calming her frayed nerves. Glancing at the clock, she made quick calculations, then pulled

the rug over her and closed her eyes. An hour of rest
might restore her.

She sank away into peaceful oblivion, her body heavy
with exhaustion.

There was a huge empty ballroom, and Ramsey was
standing in the middle of it, tall and imposing, his eyes
thunderous. She was trying to walk up to him, but no
matter how many steps she took, she wasn't coming any
closer. The space between them kept stretching with every
step, and the look on his face grew increasingly furious.

"I'm trying!" she cried, feeling tears of frustration
running down her cheeks. "Don't you know I'm trying?"
More than anything she wanted to reach him, touch him,
explain everything to him, but some terrible force was
holding her back. If only she could take hold of his hand
and look into his eyes he would understand. But he was
too far away.

"I'm leaving," he said. "It's too late." He turned his
back and strode away, turning off the lights as he left
the room.

"Don't go!" she called after him. "Please, don't leave
me!" But the door closed behind him and she was alone
in the cavernous darkness of the room.

She stopped running and collapsed to the floor, closing
her eyes. Everything was dark—the room, her heart, her
soul. She felt nothing. She knew she was never going to
feel anything again. Silence and darkness—how peaceful
it was!

Something tried to drag her out of sleep. Her mind
began to stir and she fought against it, her body re-
belling, not wanting to move. The sedation of sleep was
too comforting, yet she succumbed to the irresistible need
to open her eyes.

A face was looking down at her. A familiar face. Dark
eyes, dark hair. Ramsey. For a moment she thought she
was still dreaming. She tried to move, but her limbs were
heavy with fatigue and she just lay there staring up at
him, her mind fuzzy with sleep and confusion.

"You were sleeping," he said, stating the obvious. He stood near the couch, towering over her. "For a moment there I was concerned."

If she'd ever felt at a disadvantage, this was it. She couldn't think; her brain was mush. All the phrases and sentences she'd carefully practiced over the past two days dissolved into nothingness.

Struggling her unwilling limbs into a sitting position, she wiped her hair out of her eyes and ran her tongue over her dry lips. "Why are you here?" Her voice sounded husky, uncertain. Oh, Lord, what was this? Had she overslept?

"We're going out to a dinner party tonight," he reminded her.

"I know, I know. I was going to get ready.... What time is it?" She glanced at the clock. It was just after six. She groaned. "Oh, no! I'm sorry." She'd slept for more than two hours. "I'll get ready fast." She tried to come to her feet, but his hand pushed her back down.

"What's going on here?" he demanded.

She swallowed. "Nothing. I just fell asleep, that's all." She felt terribly on the defensive. This was not the way she had expected this confrontation to take place, with her half-unconscious, wearing a sweatsuit and her hair all over the place. This did not look good. If she wanted to get back into Ramsey's good graces, this was not the way to do it. She was supposed to look glamorous and gorgeous and ready for another evening among the jet-setters. Instead, she looked more dead than alive. She felt more dead than alive.

"Your back door was open," he stated. "Anybody could have walked in here and you would never have noticed."

So that was how he had gotten into the house. It hadn't even occurred to her to wonder about it. "Why didn't you ring the bell?" she asked.

"I did, and you didn't answer. I knocked and still no answer."

"I didn't hear the bell." She'd been dead to the world. She could have easily slept for the rest of the night right there on the couch. Only now she had to wake up and get ready. She ran her hands through her hair. "I'll run through the shower..."

"Forget it," he said curtly.

"It's late!"

"Forget the dinner." He turned away.

Samantha watched his back, and she felt suddenly very cold. So this was it. She'd messed it all up royally. But why then had he come here? She rubbed her face. She still couldn't think. Nothing made sense, and a terrible fear ran like liquid through her veins.

Ramsey walked out of the front door. He was leaving. He was furious because of what she had done, no doubt about it.

A moment later he was back, carrying the coffee decanter from the limousine. He took two mugs from the kitchen and poured them each a cup.

"Here," he said, "this will make you feel better."

"Thank you," she said, taking the cup greedily. She didn't know what was happening, or why he was here.

"What about dinner?" she asked. "Am I fired?"

One dark brow raised in surprise. "I didn't hire you, and we're not going to the dinner. I called in my apologies from the car phone."

"I'm sorry, it's all my fault. I'm sorry about Friday night, but I just didn't have a choice." Why was she apologizing, for heaven's sake? She'd done the best she could, that was all there was to it. She'd tried to be back in time for tonight, and it could have killed her. Why did she suddenly feel close to tears?

Because she was overtired from driving through the storm, because she couldn't think straight, because everything was falling apart, because she was going to lose the money for ACTION. Because she knew she looked terrible, and she wished she could get into the shower and get her head cleared up.

"Drink your coffee and stop apologizing." He drank his own coffee.

She straightened and looked right at him. "You'd better just tell me and get it out of the way."

"Tell you what?"

"Whatever you came here to tell me. Where I stand, what you expect of me, what you want. When I called you on Friday you weren't at all satisfied with the way I'd handled my problem. It's the best I could do. And if—"

"One thing I didn't expect from you was you driving back here through a damn storm!" he snapped, jamming his hands in his pockets.

"Oh, really?" she snapped back. Tension filled the room. "I thought your events were more important than anything! As far as you're concerned, your wishes need to be taken care of or else! You made that abundantly clear on Friday. I'm not stupid, Ramsey, I..." Her voice broke. She clenched her teeth together, forcing her tears back. She'd be damned if she sat there and cried in front of him.

"You didn't tell me what the problem was," he said grimly.

"Oh, I didn't, did I? As if you cared! As long as I wasn't sick or kidnapped, you didn't want to hear about it! You told me to organize, manage and delegate. Well, I did—and managed myself right into a winter storm! Don't you dare tell me you wouldn't have expected me to do that!" She took a deep shuddering breath. "And let me be perfectly clear. I didn't race back here because I care about your stupid social obligations, or to please you or whatever." She paused. "I did it for the money."

"Of course," he said evenly. "Now drink your coffee."

She had the terrible urge to throw the coffee in his face, but instead, to her horror, a sob broke loose and tears began to run down her face. Anger, the lack of sleep, the frightening drive back home, had taken their toll on her self-control. "Damn you!" she sobbed, spilling coffee on the rug as her trembling hand reached over to set the cup on the table.

"Samantha?"

She felt his hand on her shoulder and she stiffened. "Leave me alone! Go away!"

He was next to her on the couch. "I'm sorry," he said, his arm sliding around her back. "I didn't mean to make you cry. I'm a selfish bastard."

All she could do was cry some more. Something had broken inside her and she couldn't make herself stop. "I...never...cry!" she sobbed furiously. It was humiliating, embarrassing, and she knew she must look like a witch with her hair all over the place and her makeup smeared.

Ramsey drew her against his chest, wrapping both his arms snugly around her. "In that case, go ahead and let it all out," he said.

She strained against his embrace. "Leave me alone!" she whispered furiously.

"Not on your life," he said. "I started it, I'll finish it."

There was no fighting him. She felt overwhelmed with emotions, and the tears kept coming. He handed her a box of tissues, and, after she'd mopped up her face, he pulled her right back against him. Her tears spent, the anger somehow washed away, she became aware of other, more subtle sensations.

The warmth of his body, the scent of his skin, the feel of his hand stroking her hair. She lay limp against him, eyes closed. Against her cheek she felt the solid beat of his heart, the gentle rise and fall of his chest.

She didn't want to move. She didn't want his arms to release her. Never before had she felt such comfort from a man. Yet beyond the sense of comfort other feelings stirred. She was aware of her body, every inch of it, as if suddenly every single nerve end was sensitive to his touch. A heady, tingling warmth spread all through her.

It was difficult to sit still. She took in an unsteady breath and moved her head, feeling warm skin beneath her cheek. Her face was against his neck and her heart began to throb painfully. She wanted to move her lips against him, wanted to move her hands over his body. The surge of desire, the almost mindless need that threatened to take over, alarmed her. Minutes ago she had been angry, telling him to leave her alone. What was happening now? What was this madness of conflicting emotions? She tried to pull away, but he relaxed his hold on her only enough to lift her face to his.

His mouth closed over hers in gentle possession, his hands cradling her head. She closed her eyes, no longer wanting to fight or think, just letting herself be carried away by the warm, moist seduction of his mouth. A kiss, it was only a kiss. So why was she trembling? Why was her heart racing?

And then it was over.

"Better now?" he asked, releasing her face abruptly and leaning back against the couch.

Feeling cold and bereft, Samantha hugged herself, afraid to look into his eyes. She swallowed, fighting for composure. *Better now*? As if he'd kissed away a small child's pain. She glanced up now, seeing his face, but there was nothing there to see—no passion, no laughter, as if whatever he might have felt in those few moments of tenderness had been hidden away in some invisible place.

She came to her feet, forcing back her own treacherous feelings. "I'm sorry I fell apart," she said as calmly as she could. "It's not something I'm in the habit of doing. Now, if you'll excuse me, I have some restoration work to do."

The mirror in her bedroom confirmed her suspicions. She looked ravaged, her face puffy, her mascara smeared, her hair disheveled. She sighed. She looked terrible. And he had actually kissed her. Such courage. She stared at herself and despite everything she couldn't suppress a grin. The man deserved a medal.

She stripped off her sweatsuit and had a quick shower. Nothing but a full-scale repair job would have any effect.

Standing under the warm water, she realized she was feeling much better. Embarrassing as they were, tears could be a good purge. Also the strong coffee had revived her.

Maybe he would have left by the time she got back in the living room. She hoped so. No, she didn't.

She dressed in a colorful caftan with embroidery along the neck. She brushed out her hair, leaving it hanging loose around her shoulders, and put on some makeup. She surveyed herself in the mirror, seeing the color in her face and the brightness of her eyes.

She closed her eyes and sighed. What's the matter with me? she wondered.

You *know* what the matter is.

She went back into the living room, finding Ramsey scowling at the TV screen. "Bad news?" she asked casually, determined to appear in control.

He shrugged and switched it off. "Incompetence and ignorance never fail to amaze me." He patted the seat next to him. "Sit down. Tell me, how are all those ailing relatives of yours?"

She stared at him in surprise.

"Melissa told me all about it," he explained. "She seemed to think I was quite an unreasonable tyrant."

You acted like one, she wanted to say, but swallowed the words. She sat down. "My relatives are all still sick, but getting better. Lee Ann's mother came this morning, so I could leave." She looked at the front of his white dress shirt. It was no longer immaculate.

"I ruined your shirt," she said. "It's got mascara all over it."

He shrugged. "I'll live. Are you hungry?"

She frowned. "I suppose I am. I didn't have lunch."

He came to his feet. "I'll send Simon to find us some food."

"You don't have to. I'll make myself a sandwich."

"I know I don't have to, but I'll do it anyway."

"You must have better things to do," she said.

His brows lifted. "Such as what?"

"Work. Build a couple of bridges. Call Tokyo, or Singapore. It's Monday there."

"It's too early. They're still asleep or eating breakfast. Don't want to disturb them while they're eating their noodles."

"Noodles for breakfast?" she queried.

"In Singapore, anyway. Very tasty." He moved to the door. "So, do you have any dinner preferences?"

She shook her head. "No."

Ramsey went out to talk to Simon and Samantha busied herself tending the fire.

"Interesting dress," he said, coming back into the room. He touched the edge of the embroidered sleeve. "African, isn't it?"

"Yes. A friend of mine went on business to Senegal. He brought it back for me."

The phone rang and she jumped up to answer it. It was Jason, an old friend dating back to high school, calling to tell her he'd received a big promotion on Friday and had tried all weekend to contact her.

"I was out of town. Jason, this is great! Congratulations."

"I'm having a party tonight to celebrate," he said. "Can you come?"

"Oh, I'm sorry, no—I can't make it. Listen, I'll cook you dinner some night."

"No, no, I'll take you out, to celebrate. I'm rich now. I'll find an upscale place and impress you severely."

Samantha bit her lip and tried not to laugh. After where I've been lately, impressing me is going to be a challenge, she said silently. "I'm looking forward to it," she told him.

"I may even ask you again to marry me. Now that I have money you may want to reconsider."

"Don't count on it, but the dinner I'll take."

"I may never ask again, Samantha. You'd better know what you're doing. I'm going to make tons of money."

"Go back to your party, Jason," she said.

"All right, all right. I wish you were here."

"Me too. Congratulations again. Have fun."

She replaced the receiver, still smiling.

"Another friend," Ramsey said, studying her face. "Or was it the one who gave you this dress?"

"Jason? Oh, no, he's somebody else. We played opposite each other in our senior high school play. He asks me to marry him at least once a year. He called to say he'd just got a big promotion, so he thought he'd try it again."

"So why don't you marry him?"

She gave a casual shrug. "I have this romantic notion that I should love the man I marry."

"You have a lot of friends," he stated.

"I guess I do. I grew up here. That helps." It was true, she did have lots of friends, men as well as women. She was grateful for all the love and companionship, but she ached sometimes for something more. She wanted a man in her life just for herself. A man to love and be loved by.

The doorbell rang, and Ramsey came to his feet. "That must be Simon."

She had expected fast food—hamburgers, Chinese food, Mexican tacos, pizza, but not the elegant feast Simon carried in, complete with tablecloth, plates, wineglasses and wine, all of it supplied by a Leesburg restaurant.

Simon, a man of many talents, swiftly swept the coffee table clear of books and assorted items, draped the white tablecloth over it and proceeded to set out the dishes. Samantha tried not to look impressed, which was difficult, because she was, indeed, very much impressed. At the same time, the little show was appealing to her sense of humor. To have this display of glamour in her little house, to see this tall handsome man in his evening jacket standing by the stove, waiting for his chauffeur to be finished with his duties, could only make her want to laugh. It was like something out of a movie.

She tried to straighten her face. "Where's the waiter?" she asked. "Didn't they have one to spare?"

Simon stroked the back of his silver head and looked at Ramsey, then back at Samantha. "I thought perhaps you'd rather do without one, ma'am," he said evenly.

She bit her lip, then gave up and grinned at him. "I'll try to manage without one, Simon. Thank you."

He inclined his head, his face professionally blank, but the glint in his eyes gave him away. He turned and left the house.

Samantha parked herself on a chair and studied all the luscious food. "And I was expecting a pizza or something like that," she said. "Silly me."

Ramsey raised his brows. "Why have a pizza when you can have this?"

Why indeed. "It does look wonderful," she told him.

It tasted wonderful too, and she enjoyed the meal thoroughly.

"What did you think of Melissa?" she asked.

"She's a loyal friend," he said smoothly.

"So she is. We've been best friends since kindergarten, and I'm very close to her family. They tell me I'm their adopted daughter."

The dessert was raspberry torte with cream. She fought briefly with the temptation, then succumbed. The alternative was dumping it in the garbage, and that surely was a sin.

"I'm sorry you had to miss your party tonight," she said when they'd finished eating. Simon had packed everything back into the limo and they were drinking a last cup of coffee.

"Well, I'm not. I enjoy being here." Ramsey glanced at his watch and pushed himself to his feet. "Well, I'd better go."

She looked at the clock and nodded solemnly. "I suppose so. The Far East is done with its noodles."

He gave a half smile. "Right."

She came to her feet too. "I'll see you Tuesday, then."

"Yes." His hand reached out and touched her hair, his eyes holding hers.

Samantha swallowed, and the simple touch sent a wave of longing rushing through her. She saw his face come closer, like a slow-motion film, and it wasn't the face she was so familiar with, the face that showed no emotion, the face that was always reserved and controlled. The lines were softer, his eyes darker. She felt his breath fan her cheek and then his mouth touched hers in the briefest of kisses.

"Good night, Samantha," he said softly. He turned, and, without another word, left the house.

CHAPTER SEVEN

SAMANTHA wasn't Cinderella, but, when she was with Ramsey, life seemed, in many ways, like a fairy tale. And whether Ramsey agreed with it or not, she found him quite a prince. She had to admit that she liked being with him, that she enjoyed dressing up in beautiful dresses, that she even found a certain fun in watching the people at the parties and benefits.

And she liked the way he treated her when they attended the various functions—the way he smiled at her and put his arm around her, holding her close. Yet she had to remind herself that it was all part of the Big Act—nothing but a scheme to keep the vultures away. Yet at times it seemed so real that she had trouble believing it was only pretense.

Amazing how easy it all is now, she thought one night as they left the Grand Hotel after one more evening of glitz and glamour. She felt more comfortable now that she knew what to expect. Once she had decided not to let herself be intimidated she was able to relax.

The air was cold and damp, and they were hustled into the warm interior of the waiting limousine in seconds.

"Another drink?" Ramsey asked as they settled themselves in the back of the limousine.

She shook her head. "No, I've had enough."

He glanced at his watch, then turned on the small TV. "Do you mind?" he asked, switching channels. "Someone I know will be on this talk show."

"The holidays are a very difficult time for many people," someone said, a woman with a long, pointed nose. "Loneliness and depression are very commonplace, and—'' Ramsey turned off the sound. ''Sorry. I'll just keep an eye on it like this until she comes on.''

''I don't mind.'' Samantha waved at the silent image on the TV. ''It's sad so many people don't enjoy the holidays.''

''You don't suffer from loneliness and depression, I've noticed,'' he said, smiling faintly.

''Oh, no, I love the holidays. It's a magic time.''

''What are you doing at Christmas? Staying home?''

She laughed. ''My friends wouldn't allow me. I've been invited to spend it with Melissa and her family.''

He nodded. ''That's right—I remember you telling me.''

''Paul and Lee Ann wanted me to come too, but I was there for Thanksgiving. And another friend invited me too.''

''For somebody without parents, brothers or sisters, you don't seem alone in the world.''

''Well, I'm not. I'm a very lucky person.''

There was a silence as he observed her quietly.

Samantha wondered where he would spend the holidays. Alicia was going to Canada, to her in-laws. ''What about you?'' she asked. ''Are you going to spend Christmas with family? Your mother in Hawaii?''

His mouth turned down. ''I don't think so. My mother just remarried for the fourth time and her Christmas dinner is going to be a publicity event staged on the beach.''

''That's awful,'' she said impulsively. ''That's not Christmas at all.''

''Right,'' he agreed.

''So what are you going to do about Christmas?''

''I may fly out to Saint Barlow—that's a tiny island in the Caribbean. I have a house there. I'll spend time with friends, go sailing and swimming, play tennis. Relax for a day or so.''

She looked at him, but his face was inscrutable. She felt a sudden urge to reach out and touch his hand. She had the unmistakable feeling that he didn't go to the island to celebrate Christmas; he went there to escape it. In the tropics, with everything green and blooming, it would be easy to pretend Christmas was just another day.

Not that he'd admit it. Not that she could even begin to mention her suspicion. She met his eyes and smiled. "You mean you actually take a day off?" she asked lightly.

He smiled now, too. "Isn't it amazing?"

She nodded. "I can't imagine you in anything but a business suit. You'll be wearing shorts and shirts, and even a bathing suit?"

Humor gleamed in his eyes. "Maybe you should come along and see for yourself."

He was teasing her, which was amazing. To her horror, she felt color creep into her face.

"I'll take your word for it." The sudden thought of him wearing nothing but a bathing suit was hopelessly exciting, and her composure deserted her completely.

He watched her, his smile deepening. He reached out suddenly, putting the palm of his hand against her cheek. "I don't believe this," he said. "You're actually blushing!"

His touch did nothing to calm her. Her heart leaped frantically. "Don't be ridiculous! Why would I be blushing?"

"I have no idea," he said lightly, and lowered his hand.

Neither do I, she wanted to say, but the words didn't come. To her relief, Ramsey returned his attention to the TV.

"Here she is." He switched the sound back on. The woman being introduced was a small blonde with deep blue eyes and a lovely tan, by the name of Daniella Michaels.

"I know her," Samantha said. "She's the painter, the one who lives in Africa. We went to the opening of her exhibit at the Benedict."

"You remember," he remarked.

"Of course I remember. I loved her paintings, they're so bold and brilliant." She turned her attention back to the screen, listening to the interview. One of Daniella's paintings had been auctioned off at a benefit, the proceeds going to a small orphanage on Saint Barlow.

Surprised, Samantha looked at Ramsey. "Saint Barlow?"

"It's a small world. Hayden Penbrooke, her father-in-law, and my father were friends. They have a house on the island too."

"Alicia told me about the orphanage. Have you seen it?"

"Many times." He gave her a probing look, and for a moment it seemed he was going to say something more, then changed his mind.

They listened in silence to the rest of the interview. Samantha wondered if she should ask him about the children coming to Philadelphia for medical treatment, but her instincts told her he might not be overjoyed knowing Alicia had talked about him, so she remained silent. Looking away, she glanced out of the window into the dark night.

"It's snowing!" she exclaimed. "Look!" Thick, fat snowflakes drifted to the ground.

"So it is," said Ramsey, switching off the television.

"They said this morning it was going to miss us."

"They were wrong." He pressed the button of the intercom and spoke briefly to Simon, then turned to her. "He's been listening to the weather report. They're expecting six to eight inches and they've got several inches farther west already. Simon suggested we turn back to my place. It makes no sense to try and make it to Aurora tonight. You'd better stay with me."

"I won't be teaching tomorrow anyway," she said. "With that kind of snow the schools will be closed." In a rural county with many narrow back roads that didn't get plowed right away, the school buses couldn't make it through.

"They sure blew this forecast," said Ramsey, watching the snowflakes coming down in a thick, lacy veil of white.

Samantha grinned. "I don't mind—I love snow. I love seeing everything all covered with snow—all the trees and bushes and houses. Like a fairy-tale land." She paused, aware that he was watching her with amusement. "I hope the roads will be clear enough tomorrow so Simon can take me home."

"Anything you need to be back for?" he asked.

She smiled into his eyes. "Yes. I want to play in the snow with the kids in the neighborhood." She straightened her face. "The kids count on me, you see. They always come and get me when it snows. We make snowmen and igloos and we have snowball fights. And then after we're all thoroughly stiff and frozen, they all come in and I make a big fire and we have hot chocolate. It's a tradition. My grandmother started it."

"You wouldn't want to disappoint them," he said.

"Certainly not," she said primly, and laughed.

The limousine drew up to the apartment building and Simon helped her out. The air was cold and clear and tinglingly fresh, and already the world was covered with a thin white veil. She moved out from under the canopy that ran from the building to the curb and stood in the snow, drawing her wrap tightly around her shoulders, and inhaled deeply. "Snow smells wonderful," she said.

Ramsey took her arm. "Come inside before you freeze to death in that dress."

"Just a minute, please! It's so gorgeous out here, so clean and pristine. Think of it, everything is covered up, dirt and sins and ugliness." She glanced at him. He was watching her again, always watching with that strange look on his face. "Don't you see it?" she asked.

He nodded. "Yes."

"When I was little I used to think heaven must be like this—all new and clean and pure." She took in another deep breath. "It's like champagne! Come on, taste it." She looked at him, challenging him. "Take a deep breath, taste the air."

His eyes in hers, he took in a deep breath, releasing it very slowly.

She watched him, the big man in his formal evening clothes, snow on his black hair, breathing in the air, and a longing swept over her. She wanted more than anything to wipe away the seriousness. She wanted to break through the reserve. She wanted the warmth that lay behind that cool, composed surface of his control, the warmth that she saw glowing behind the rare smile in his eyes. She wanted to hear him laugh out loud, to see him relaxed and easygoing, to see him away from other people who talked business or politics with him. Away from his phone and his sterile, unhomey penthouse apartment where everything was too beautiful, too perfect.

She put her hand on his arm. "Come with me tomorrow morning," she said. "Come play in the snow with me."

She heard her own voice, the words floating softly in the snowy silence around them, and they surprised her. They'd come of their own accord.

She saw her own surprise reflected in his eyes. Snowflakes clung briefly to his lashes, then melted. Not a sound came from anywhere. No wind stirred the heavy snow-laden branches. It was a fairy-tale night and nothing seemed quite real, not least the words that had come from her unbidden.

"Come play in the snow with you?" he repeated on a low note.

She let her hand drop away from his arm. "Yes."

A smile glimmered in his dark eyes. "That's an irresistible invitation."

"But it's Wednesday, and you have to work come hell or high water."

"Right. But not if it snows."

She stared at him. "Really? You mean . . ."

He gave a crooked smile. "I'm the boss. I decide." He put his arm around her and drew her close. "Now we really must go up, or you'll catch something."

He led her into the building. In the warm elevator, she shivered suddenly, feeling for the first time how cold she was, realizing too that he still had his arm around her.

"You'd better have something hot to drink to warm you up," he said as they entered the apartment.

The view from the large windows was stunning. A snowy panorama sparkling with diamond lights.

"Sit here," he said, pushing a chair near the windows. "I'll get us something."

She sat, drinking in the view, still shivering a little. Ramsey came back a while later, carrying a tray with two mugs.

"Hot chocolate?" She looked at him, surprised, taking the hot mug in her cold hands. She sipped greedily from the hot drink. "There's something in it," she said.

"Rum," he said. "To help the warming process."

"It's delicious."

He pulled up another chair, close to hers, and they watched the view in companionable silence, drinking the chocolate. It made her warm and drowsy, and looking at him she felt the longing steal through her again, the need to feel his arms around her again, to feel the beating of his heart. It was always there, that sweet pain, hiding on the edges of her consciousness.

The drink finished, she came slowly to her feet. "Thank you, that was very nice."

He came to his feet too, standing very close, his dark eyes looking down into hers. Her heart began to pound. She bit her lip, remembering the way he had kissed her before, wishing he would kiss her now.

"Good night, Samantha." He was smiling, the severe lines of his angular face softened.

Her heart lurched into a frantic rhythm. She felt an aching need to reach out and touch him, to feel him close, and it seemed to her she saw the same yearning in the depths of his eyes. For an endless, breathless moment their eyes locked and the silence quivered with tension. She forgot to breathe and for a delirious instant she thought he really was going to kiss her. Then he drew back, almost imperceptibly, and disappointment washed over her.

"Good night," she said, her voice low and husky. Turning, she walked quickly out of the room.

Her dreams that night were filled with mixed-up images of tropical beaches covered with snow, of waving coconut palms, and the two of them in swimsuits in the water.

Ramsey was holding her and kissing her. "Samantha," he said softly, "I don't love you, you know that, don't you?"

When she awoke she was crying.

A snowball hit Ramsey square in the back. "Hey, mister, you're dead!"

Ramsey grabbed Samantha's arm and, buckling his legs, dragged her with him as he dropped himself in the snow amid cheers of victory from the army of young children.

As soon as they'd arrived at Samantha's house earlier that morning, the children had come out of the woodwork, dressed in bright snow clothes, ready to play. And play they had, for a couple of hours at least.

Samantha lay in the snow, her face buried against Ramsey's padded shoulder. She squirmed and lifted it away, amazed at his reaction, his immediate surrender to the childish game. Perhaps it was the unselfconsciousness of the children that made it easy for him to take part in their play. They didn't know him, didn't expect anything of him but that he play.

"Don't look so surprised," he told her. "I can play dead like the best of them."

The next moment small bodies were on top of them, squirming, laughing.

"He's dead! They're both dead! We gotta bury them!"

Ramsey opened his eyes and looked at Samantha. "That's a bloodthirsty crew you've got here," he remarked.

"Don't blame me. I didn't raise them."

"Must be the TV. And the video games."

Small hands started piling snow on top of them.

"They're not really—"

"Of course they are. Now lie still and play dead."

Which was easier said than done, Samantha realized. They were lying close together, legs and bodies touching, his arm around her, his face almost touching. The warmth of his breath fanned her cheek. She wondered what had made him come with her this morning. Sometimes he surprised her. She sensed in him a searching, a need for something he might not fully understand himself. She felt his body shift against hers. Laughing lights danced in his eyes. She loved the carefree expression of his face.

"Remember those kids we saw by the bridge that day we went to Richard's house for lunch?" he whispered from the corner of his mouth.

"Yes."

"You were right."

"About what?"

"About feeling the cold. I don't feel the cold."

"That's because of those fancy ski clothes you're wearing," she told him.

"You think?"

"Positively."

"What about you?"

"I'm freezing."

He laughed, which got an immediate reminder from the snow-scooping children that he was supposed to be dead and therefore should not laugh.

Samantha was not freezing and he knew it. Neither was she dead. She felt more alive now than ever before. Half-covered with snow, surrounded by children, she was acutely aware of his nearness, as if all the distraction around them was taking place in another reality.

They were covered up to their necks with snow. The children shouted and danced around them in some sort of primitive victory dance.

She couldn't take it any longer. Ramsey's face was too close, his body touching hers. She wanted to kiss him. She dared not look into his eyes for fear he would read her thoughts. She turned her face away from him and drew in an unsteady breath. "Who wants hot chocolate and a doughnut?" she called out.

They all cheered.

She began to struggle out from under the load of snow. For an instant Ramsey's arm tightened around her and she turned to meet his eyes.

"Chicken," he whispered.

He stood by the door, his hand on the knob. The children had gone and the house was quiet again. "Thanks for the snow play," he said. "Very refreshing."

She smiled. "You're very welcome."

He gave her a long, silent look and hesitation flickered briefly in his eyes.

"You should have children of your own," he said softly.

Samantha's heart contracted. "I'd like that," she said. "But I'll have to find myself a husband first. I'd rather like doing it the traditional way."

He was silent for a moment. "And you think you're going to find one out here?" he asked then.

"What's wrong with here?" Why did she suddenly feel so defensive? So angry?

Because you don't want to think of a husband and children. Because all you think about these days is Ramsey, and he isn't husband material.

He shrugged. "The suburbs are full of married men, and outside of them, here, in the country—" he waved his hand "—what have you got here? More married people, old folks, married farmers, a few societal dropouts. You aren't going to find anyone here."

"I like it here," she said stubbornly. "So maybe I'll grow up to be an eccentric spinster teacher."

"Knitting sweaters, baby-sitting other people's children and carting bags of food to the hungry."

Anger swept through her. Or maybe it wasn't really anger. It was more fear that he was right, that perhaps she would never find someone to share her life with, fear that she might never feel about another man the way she felt about him. And he, of course, was not on the market.

"I can think of worse things," she said, feeling her body tense. "Anyway, what do you care? I'm only a temporary employee, and when the holiday season is over you won't need me any more and you'll never see me again. No need to worry."

She was saying the words more to herself than to him. She had to get used to the idea, harden herself against her own feelings. After all, this was the way it was going to be.

He studied her silently, his face unrevealing. "True," he said then, and, turning abruptly, walked out of the door and was gone.

She sank down on a chair, feeling as if her heart had been ripped out.

On Sunday evening there was a benefit concert, and afterward Ramsey took her to a small, out-of-the-way restaurant for a late dinner.

It was the first time they had been out alone in public. Always there were other people—business acquaintances, friends, although none of them seemed very close, except sometimes the women who seemed to want to touch Ramsey, or make other proprietorial gestures towards him.

It seemed a little strange not to have other people around, but she liked it. She could relax and didn't need to worry about what to say or not to say.

They'd ordered their meal and were sipping their drinks, when Ramsey reached into his inside breast pocket and took something out.

He handed it to her across the table.

"Here," he said. "I'd like you to have this."

CHAPTER EIGHT

SAMANTHA looked at the check, then back up at Ramsey. His face revealed nothing.

"I don't understand," she said. "Why are you giving me this?"

Ramsey picked up his glass and took a drink. "I want you to have it. I want you to spend it on yourself."

She stared at the check in her hands, at the bold handwriting, the large signature. It was a huge amount of money, at least for her. Was he feeling sorry for her? Did he think she was poor, living in her small house, eating root soup and chopping her own wood?

She wasn't poor. She could live in the suburbs in a condo townhouse with central heating if she wanted to. She had a good job and she was doing just fine, thank you.

"I don't need it," she said.

"It's not a matter of needing it. It's a matter of just having it and spending it." He gave a crooked little smile. "Frivolously, preferably."

She shook her head slowly. "No, Ramsey, I don't want it. I can't accept it." Not even to do frivolous things.

"I insist, Samantha." He met her eyes with quiet determination. "It's time somebody gave you something."

She gave him a look of surprise. "I don't know what you mean."

"You give of yourself all the time. Giving is all you do. You spend hours working for ACTION, worrying about other people, taking them food and blankets and finding them jobs and houses to live in. And you traipse off to Philadelphia to take care of sick relatives, and God knows what else that's escaped my attention."

She gave a frustrated sigh. "Ramsey, I *like* doing that! Besides, I'm hardly doing it by myself. Do me a favor, don't make me sound like some martyr, please!"

He took a drink from his wine. "I'd just like to give you something, Samantha. What's wrong with that?"

She shook her head. "Nothing in principle, I suppose, but you're already giving a big donation to ACTION. That's what the agreement was."

"This isn't about business."

She bit her lip. "If it isn't business, then what is it?" She felt her heart suddenly race, she wasn't sure why.

"It's personal. Just a personal gift from me to you, very simple."

Personal. She looked at his face, wondering what went on in his mind. Personal. From all evidence he was not interested in the personal. No, that wasn't entirely true. He seemed interested enough in wanting to know about her. He just didn't want her to know about him. And all of it was temporary.

"You don't have to give me anything." He owed her nothing.

"I *want* to give you something."

"So give me a box of Godiva chocolates," she said, feeling the little devil inside her begin to stir. "Chocolates I can handle."

He was a master at controlling his facial expression, but she'd caught him off guard. The surprise was clearly visible in his face.

"You don't want this check, but you'll take a box of chocolates?"

She gave him a wide-eyed, innocent look, trying not to laugh. "Yes, a big one."

Ramsey leaned back in his chair and studied her silently.

Samantha flattened the check on the tablecloth. "I still don't understand why you want me to have this."

There was a silence. He fingered the stem of his glass, his gaze settling on the swirling liquid. Then he slowly raised his gaze to meet her eyes. "You make me feel good,

Samantha," he said quietly. "I'm enjoying your company. You make me laugh. I just want to give you something back."

She stared at him. She could not believe her ears, and then a strange emotion washed over her—sadness mixed with an unaccountable tenderness.

"You don't pay people money for making you feel good, Ramsey. It comes for free."

He said nothing, his face blank, as if suddenly he had gone into hiding.

"You think everything is for sale," she said softly. "You think if you want something, you pay for it. If you have enough money, you can have whatever you want. You think that if people do something for you or give you something, they expect something in return." She looked at his face, biting her lip. "Well, you're wrong, Ramsey. Sometimes people are nice to you just because they want to, and sometimes people give of themselves just for the joy of it." She took the check, folded it carefully and slipped it under his hand.

"I don't want your money, Ramsey."

Ramsey took her home after they'd finished eating, since she had to teach school the next day. She'd enjoyed dinner and no further mention of the money had been made.

He walked her to the door, taking the key from her fingers and opening it for her.

"Would you like to come in for another cup of coffee?" she asked. She felt awkward and she didn't know why.

He glanced at his watch. "I can't, I'm expecting a call from Hong Kong."

"Thank you for dinner," she said. It sounded more formal than she intended.

"I'm the one to say thank you," he returned, and, before she realized what was happening, he had drawn her into his arms, and his mouth, firm and urgent, was on hers. For a moment she stood motionless in his embrace, her heart thudding, then on instinct, she put her arms around his neck and yielded to him, opening her mouth to his.

He made an inarticulate sound in his throat and his kiss grew hungrier, his tongue inviting hers to an erotic dance of desire, and a flood of tingling, dizzy need swept through her.

She clung to him, wanting nothing more than to forget everything, to give herself up to this mindless longing, yet in the back of her mind some shred of sanity held out while her senses reeled.

Don't *do* this to me! she wanted to cry. Please don't make me feel this way. I don't know what to do about it.

In another two weeks it would all be over. What was she going to do with all the feelings and emotions he had stirred up inside her? What was she going to do with all those painful longings she had no control over? She wanted to make love. She'd never wanted a man the way she wanted him.

She tried to pull back, and he released her slowly, his breathing ragged, his eyes searching her face in the shadowed darkness surrounding them.

The wind felt icy on her heated cheeks. The bare branches of the trees swayed back and forth against the dark, starless sky, and dry, dead leaves rustled across the drive.

"Good night, Samantha." He turned and strode back to the limousine.

Samantha went inside and closed the door, barely able to breathe. Her legs shook and she sank down onto the couch and hugged herself.

What was it that he wanted from her?

It was the question that haunted her through a restless night and all through the next day. With her mind in turmoil it was hard to concentrate on perfectly formed *h*s and *g*s. The children seemed restless, but maybe that was only because they were reacting to her absent-mindedness.

All during the day the words Ramsey had spoken kept coming back to her as if somehow there was a message in them she failed to recognize. "It's personal," he'd said. "I just want to give you something back."

He felt she was giving him something and he felt beholden. He wasn't used to being on the receiving end of relationships, no doubt. Always he was the dispenser of money, presents and favors, and he liked to keep the books balanced.

Only she didn't understand why he felt he was in her debt. What was it that he thought she was giving him? Nothing she was even aware of. "You make me feel good...you make me laugh." She was just being herself, and there were no strings attached and he knew it. It bothered him. He knew what to do with strings and conditions and agreements. He knew how to buy people and manipulate them and get the most out of every deal he made.

He was getting more out of the deal he'd made with her than he'd bargained for, was that it? Did he feel... With an impatient hand Samantha wiped the hair out of her face and concentrated on the blackboard. She wasn't going to figure him out.

Soon after she came home that afternoon, a car drove up and delivered a huge golden box of Godiva chocolates.

"I've got great instincts," Melissa said with a grin as she looked greedily at the luxurious box on Samantha's coffee table. She'd arrived minutes after it had been delivered.

"Great timing too," said Samantha.

"I've never seen a box this big. Are you going to open it?"

"No. I'm going to dip the whole thing in bronze and save it for posterity. *Of course* I'm going to open it!"

"That bow alone is worth five bucks," Melissa remarked as Samantha removed it. The lid lifted off, they stared for a moment in reverent awe at the luscious display of chocolate.

"Which one is the absolute best, do you think?" Samantha asked, trying to look serious.

"You won't know until you try them all," Melissa said promptly, looking solemn.

"Well, let's go for it."

Three chocolates later and feeling silly with the giggles, Samantha went to the kitchen and poured coffee.

"This one has nuts in it," said Melissa, biting into a fourth. "Pecans—yum, great. I rate this one a nine." She looked up, eyes narrowed. "Why did Ramsey give this to you? Did you sleep with him?"

"No!"

"Phew, that's a relief."

"You're just jealous. You want him for yourself."

"I don't want him, he's too cool for me. I just want his money."

Samantha bit into another chocolate. "Well, I'd take him without his money."

Melissa looked up and met her eyes, saying nothing.

Samantha heard her words echoing in the silence. They'd come out without conscious thought, and the spontaneous admission was like a confession.

"You *are* in love with him."

Samantha felt herself tense. "I'll get over it."

"Why did he give you this box?"

"Because I asked him to."

Melissa's eyes widened. "You *asked* him for a box of chocolates?"

"Yes." Samantha grinned. "He gave me this huge check and I said I didn't want his money, he could give me a box of chocolates instead." She recounted the incident and Melissa listened, practically gaping at her. The story finished, Melissa was silent for a moment, looking thoughtful.

"Maybe he's trying to tell you something," she said at last.

"Like what?" Samantha took a drink from her coffee.

"He wants you. You got his hormones stirring and he figures he might as well extend the relationship into bed. He's trying to buy you, so he doesn't have to feel guilty— not that he looks like anyone who's plagued by guilt a lot."

Samantha felt her heart contract. "That's crazy," she said, not actually convinced. Could it be true?

Melissa shrugged. "Rich people do crazy things. Did you read in the paper about that rich guy building a gold-plated mausoleum for his dog? It took—"

"I read it." Samantha glanced at her watch and closed the box. "Simon will be here in half an hour. Since you're here, why don't you help me get the food deliveries ready?"

"You're going out again? Good heavens, how do you keep it up?"

"It's just a cocktail party. I'll be home early."

The cocktail party was not a big affair, but it was certainly the most boring Samantha had attended with Ramsey. Having politely listened for twenty minutes to a discussion on stocks and bonds, she escaped and went in search of the ladies' room.

It was as palatial and opulent as the rest of the hotel, with marble floors, huge tinted mirrors and a sitting area with comfortably upholstered chairs. She sat in front of the mirror and took out her lipstick, but before she had a chance to apply it, the door opened and a woman strode in.

Cecilia. She wore a black dress and diamonds as cold as her eyes.

Samantha lowered her hand, praying for composure.

"I thought it was you," said Cecilia. "I want a word with you."

Samantha raised the lipstick to her mouth and looked at her image in the mirror. "Go ahead," she said casually.

"I have some advice for you," Cecilia said. "I suggest you leave Ramsey alone. You'll save yourself a lot of grief."

"Why?"

"He's way out of your league, girl."

Samantha nodded. "You're right about that." She covered her lipstick and put it in her evening bag. "I suppose," she went on, "that you want him for yourself?"

Cecilia was momentarily taken aback, and Samantha smiled. "Oh, I don't blame you. He's rich, he's handsome, he's got all sorts of influence and power. Very sexy stuff, all that."

Cecilia's hands clenched into fists and her face took on a deeper shade of pink. Her eyes blazed. "Listen to me, you little schemer! If you know what's good for you, you'll leave him alone!"

Samantha sighed. "I try, but he won't let me. To tell you the truth, Cecilia, I don't know what he sees in me. I've got nothing to offer him. I have no money, no illustrious background, no fame." She gave Cecilia a wide-eyed look. "What do you think it is? True love, maybe?"

Cecilia's face grew rigid with barely contained rage. "You think you're so clever!" she hissed. "But don't get any ideas. In the end you'll be sorry." She turned and marched out of the room.

Samantha followed a moment later. Glancing around to find Ramsey, she saw him with Cecilia hanging on to his arm. She walked up to them, and Ramsey smiled at her and put his free arm around her. "I wondered where you were," he said.

She smiled up at him adoringly, aware of Cecilia on his other side, observing them. "I was in the ladies' room," she said. "One of your admirers attacked me and said I should leave you alone. For my own good, of course."

Dark brows raised. "Who was it?"

"A tall blonde wearing a black dress."

He jerked his head to his left to look at Cecilia, who froze into a statue.

Samantha smiled. "Oh, don't be angry with her, Ramsey. She didn't mean any harm. She said you were way out of my league and I should save myself a lot of grief. I suppose she's right, actually.''

Ramsey's face was cold as he looked at Cecilia. "I appreciate your concern for Samantha," he said, his voice frigidly polite, "but you would ingratiate yourself easier with me or others if you'd mind your own business.''

Cecilia had, by power of long practice, composed herself. "I apologize if I've upset you," she said nicely. "As Samantha said, I meant no harm. Now, if you'll excuse me, I see someone I need to speak to." She smiled. "See you.''

Samantha slowly released a long breath. Ramsey studied her and shook his head. "Good God, Samantha, you made yourself an enemy.''

"She was one from the day I met her," she told him. "And she's hardly the only one. You wanted me to keep the vultures away. Well, it's a nasty job." She looked at him and frowned. "You know, it's bringing out a nasty streak in my character. I'm not sure I like it.''

His eyes were warm as he smiled down at her, and he tightened his arm for a moment, bringing her closer to his side in a protective gesture. "Well, I like you just the way you are, nasty streak and all. Come on, you must need a drink after that little scene.''

His arm around her was more comfort than a drink could ever be, and he did not release her as they went on to mingle with the other guests. Samantha was aware of the warmth of his body as she stood close to him and tried not to think of his kiss the night before. Maybe it wasn't important. Maybe it was nothing more than a meaningless kiss that had got out of hand a little.

"He's trying to buy you, so he doesn't have to feel guilty." Melissa's words haunted her, yet she couldn't bring herself to believe they held any truth.

She was relieved when after an hour Ramsey told her it was time to go.

"I can see you didn't have the most stimulating of times," he said, as they sat down in the limousine.

"Oh, well," she said lightly, "it's all for a good cause."

He gave her a quick, sideways glance. "Yes, right." He selected a music cassette and slipped it into the tape deck. Soft classical music flowed through the air. She took her shoes off and tucked her legs underneath.

"Ramsey?" she began.

"Yes?"

Her heart began to thump nervously. "Why don't you ever want to talk about yourself?"

He shrugged. "I don't find myself a particularly interesting subject of discussion."

She bit her lip. "I'd like to know more about you."

"Why?"

She sensed his withdrawal, the almost imperceptible narrowing of his eyes, a sudden wariness.

"We're always talking about me, but you never want to talk about you. I'd just like to know more about you, what you feel, what your dreams are, what makes you happy. It's the normal thing to do between people, isn't it? We talk about ourselves, get to know each other."

He met her gaze, and his eyes were dark and unreadable. "You don't need to get to know me, Samantha," he said quietly.

She stared at him, at his face that seemed no more than a polite mask, and the hurt was so deep that she had to fight to keep tears coming into her eyes.

The next day at five, Melissa stopped by again, her car full of food donated by a local church. They put everything on the shelves in the ACTION pantry, while Melissa talked glowingly about a new patient who had had his appendix removed. He was handsome, funny and single, and was the owner of a large riding school. He was apparently so impressed with Melissa's tender loving care that he had promised to personally teach her to ride a horse as soon as he was able. Melissa admitted that she'd always wanted to learn to ride, which was news to Samantha, but she wisely refrained from commenting. It made her happy to see Melissa so enthusiastic.

The food put away, they spend some time at the kitchen table doing paperwork and discussing the families who needed help.

They were just about finished when the phone rang. It was Jeremy Kramer. Samantha had seen him several times in Washington, and she'd had a cup of coffee with him once.

"I'm doing a piece on Thai and Vietnamese restaurants," he told her. "I'm going to case out a new restaurant in Leesburg and wonder if you'd join me and tell me what you think of the food. I know this is last minute again, but I'm afraid that's how I live—everything last minute."

Samantha laughed. "Well, to tell you the truth, I'm looking at some leftover spaghetti for dinner, so how can I refuse?"

"Great. I'll pick you up at seven."

"Guess who that was," said Samantha as she replaced the receiver. "Jeremy Kramer. We're going out to eat Thai food."

Melissa gathered up the papers. "Lucky you. I have to go home and wash my uniforms." She picked up her coat and bag, and gave Samantha a quick hug. "Have fun, Sam."

The restaurant Jeremy took her to was small and unpretentious and smelled deliciously of familiar and unfamiliar spices.

"You'd better order for both of us," Samantha suggested as she glanced at the menu. "I'm no expert on Thai food—I've had it exactly once. And don't take my opinion for anything, I won't know whereof I speak."

"Let's start with the *tom yam kung*. And what would you like to drink with it? Thai beer? Wine? Tea?"

"Tea, please."

The soup was spicy and delicious and full of shrimp. They talked while they ate, an easy relaxed conversation she enjoyed as much as the food. Within the space of twenty minutes she had a good picture of Jeremy's background—his family, his misadventures as a boy, his career. Twenty minutes, and she knew more about him than she'd been able to glean from Ramsey in days.

"I heard there was a top-secret meeting between MacMillan and Crawford," he said casually, his gaze on his plate.

"I'm afraid I don't keep track of his appointments," she said lightly. She was getting better at saying things without saying anything.

Jeremy studied her. "I hope Ramsey won't mind us having dinner together," he said.

"I don't know why he should." "You don't need to get to know me, Samantha," he had said. She balanced a shrimp on her chopsticks. "This stuff is delicious, don't you think?"

"Yes, it is." He gave her a searching look. "What happened to Violet?"

Violet. She'd heard the name mentioned several times. From what she'd heard, Samantha had deduced that the woman must have had a relationship with Ramsey. But Ramsey had never mentioned her and she had no idea what had happened.

"I don't know," she said.

Jeremy frowned, stroking his beard. "Sorry— shouldn't have mentioned her."

"Why not? Who is she?"

He looked at her oddly. "I'm surprised you don't know. She was with Ramsey for quite a while. She went to Europe a couple of months ago, but nobody's heard of a breakup."

She felt an unaccountable tightness in her chest. "I have no idea. He hasn't mentioned her."

"He must have dumped her. Discreetly, of course. He's so damned discreet." Jeremy smiled and rubbed his beard. "Let me pour you some more tea."

He took her home after the meal was over, and Melissa phoned almost as soon as he had driven off.

"I warn you," Samantha told her, "I'm tired and I'm full of good food, so no disaster stories."

Melissa laughed. "No news from the ACTION front. I'm only checking up on you to make sure your rendezvous with Jeremy went all right."

"You're not curious, are you?"

"Me?" Melissa's voice was mock indignant. "No, of course not. I'm just making sure you're all right and he treated you well."

"So he did. Fed me lavishly, but didn't lay a hand on me."

"Well, good. Fast movers are not to be trusted. How was your evening otherwise?"

"Very nice. We had a good time. He's a nice guy. He's got lots of funny stories and it's easy talking with him."

"Is that all?"

"You sound disappointed." Samantha switched the receiver to her other ear. "Am I mistaken, or are you eager to see me fall for another man?"

Melissa sighed. "Oh, Sam, yes, I am. Somebody nice and ordinary and safe."

Samantha laughed—she couldn't help it. "Somebody boring and predictable, just like what you want for yourself, right?"

"Okay, okay, you know what I mean."

"I know what you mean."

"He called," Melissa said. "Ramsey, that is. He wondered if you were with me."

"What did you say?" asked Samantha.

"That you'd been invited out to dinner, and probably wouldn't be home until late." Melissa's voice was gleeful.

"You're rotten, Melissa," Samantha said. "But it won't do you any good. As long as it doesn't interfere with his precious schedule, Ramsey doesn't care if I sleep with the King of Sweden."

"I hope it stays that way. It'll be your only salvation."

Samantha groaned. "Melissa!"

"Okay, okay. I'll let you go. You'd better get your rest so you'll be up to taming the little pagans tomorrow."

Samantha wasn't tired. After she'd said good-night to Melissa, she turned on the TV and picked up her knitting. The front panel of Ramsey's sweater was finished, and she was almost done with the back. That left the sleeves. She tried not to think about Violet or about what she meant to Ramsey. Maybe he'd only needed her because Violet was gone for a few months. "You don't need to get to know me, Samantha."

It was suddenly hard to see what she was doing. The colors blurred before her eyes and she couldn't see the stitches on the knitting needles.

Something wasn't right. Every time it seemed they were moving a little closer, something happened to make him retreat. It wasn't her imagination that he seemed more open, more relaxed at times. But it never lasted. In the end he always pushed her away again.

"Oh, damn you, Ramsey," she muttered. "I wish I'd never met you."

He called the next day to say that on Friday afternoon the limo would come for her half an hour early. It needed to be back in town to go to National Airport to meet a business friend of Ramsey's. "I tried calling you yesterday," said Ramsey. "I understand you were out to dinner."

"So I was. I was out with a writer, a food writer—we were testing out a Thai restaurant. Gee, what a job!"

"I see," he said abruptly.

"Something wrong?"

"No. I'll see you on Friday, then." He hung up.

The conversation had taken all of a minute and a half, a short, businesslike exchange that could just as well have been performed by a secretary or another minor minion, or Simon, for that matter. Yet he always called himself. Samantha wondered why. On the phone he always sounded in a hurry, as if he really didn't have time to speak to her.

On Friday night the limousine picked her up early as arranged and, once at the penthouse, she took her time with a delicious lazy bath and still finished dressing with plenty of time to spare.

In the last couple of days she'd given herself an ongoing pep talk. Her feelings for Ramsey were not going to get her down. Whether Violet featured in his life or not had nothing to do with her. In two weeks this nightmare would be over and she could go on with her life—without Ramsey in it to disturb her nights and days and wreak havoc with her emotions. For now she was going to enjoy herself.

She looked around the room. There were fresh flowers on the dressing table, as there were always. Pale yellow roses this time. There were always fresh flowers in the living room and dining room as well, and she suspected there was a standing order with a florist.

The room was beginning to seem familiar now that she had slept in it a number of times. With its elegant Oriental décor, it was very different from her own bedroom with its old-fashioned brass bed and the quilt her grandmother had made. The contents of the closets, too, were very different. The large mirrored wardrobe here held all her party gowns and elegant high-heeled shoes. At home her bedroom closet was full of warm, long skirts, bright-colored short skirts, jeans, thick sweaters, boots, and sneakers.

Tonight she would be the princess and lead the glamorous life. Tomorrow morning, after the limo dropped her off at home, she'd have to do laundry, chop wood and take food to an old lady who lived alone and loved talking about the old days.

I'm leading a double life, she thought, and grinned at herself. A secret life.

She threw one last glance in the mirror, smoothing her dress over her hips. It was a lovely gown of brandy colored silk that matched her eyes, short, with small off-the-shoulder sleeves. She'd piled her hair high on her head, and put in long diamond earrings from the velvet treasure box on the dressing table.

"The sheikhs will love this thing," Alicia had said, referring to the guests at the reception for which Samantha was buying the dress.

"What about Ramsey?" Samantha had asked.

"Oh, he'll love it too. It's discreetly sexy." Alicia gave her a searching look. "How is it going between you two?"

Samantha smoothed the fabric over her hips, avoiding Alicia's eyes. "Oh, fine," she said, trying to sound casual.

"I'd hate to see you hurt," Alicia said quietly. "He's such a selfish, arrogant son of a bitch. He appears to be so self-contained, as if he doesn't need anybody, but..." She shrugged, not finishing her sentence.

"But what?" In the fitting room mirror, their eyes met.

"I think deep down he's very lonely. I think that what he needs is someone to really love him just for himself."

Samantha realized her heart was beating fast. "That's what we all need, isn't it?"

Alicia nodded, not looking at her. "Yes, of course. Here, let me help you get out of this dress. Are you going to take it?"

"I like it. Yes."

Now, in her bedroom, Samantha looked at herself wearing the dress, trying not to remember that conversation.

Discreetly sexy, Alicia had said. She lifted her chin and batted her eyelashes at herself in the mirror. Then, pirouetting on her right foot, she danced out of the door, calming into a sedate pace as she approached the living room. She peeped into the kitchen, and Mrs. Gregory noticed her and smiled.

"Come in and show me your dress," she said. "Oh, you look very beautiful."

"Thank you."

"Mr. MacMillan is in the living room. I know you're early today. How about a drink and a little snack?"

"That would be lovely. I'd like a cup of coffee, actually. Is that a problem?"

"Of course not."

Nothing was ever a problem for Mrs. Gregory. Samantha liked her. She was friendly and liked to chat, which was nice when Samantha had breakfast in the mornings. More often than not, Ramsey had already left by the time she got up. The man certainly didn't waste his time goofing off on a Saturday morning that was perfectly good for working.

Samantha swung into the living room, finding Ramsey, dressed in a dark suit, speaking into a portable phone. His back was turned toward her and she studied the long lean line of his body and the broad shoulders, his confident stance. She felt the tightening of her stomach muscles as she looked at him, and he turned around abruptly as if he'd felt her regard. His dark gaze swept over her, his mouth still talking. He broke off the conversation and put the phone on a side table.

"You have style, Samantha. Very impressive."

At his words, her heart did a joyful little dance in her chest. She curtsied, which didn't quite work with a short dress. "Thank you, sir," she said in her best Southern drawl. Though she was treating it lightly, the compliment pleased her more than she wanted to admit.

He lowered himself in a chair and picked up a thick document. "I'll be finished with this in a few minutes," he said, tapping the papers.

"Sure, no problem." She walked over to the window and looked out over the dark river for a while, turning when she heard Mrs. Gregory come in with a tray. She placed it on the table and quietly left the room. Samantha looked at Ramsey's bent head, feeling a painful weakness in her stomach. Did he love another woman? Did he love Violet? Why had he kissed her, then? If he was so intent on keeping her at a distance, why did his kisses seem so intense? "You don't need to get to know me, Samantha." Her heart contracted. It didn't make sense. Nothing made sense.

She dropped herself down on the sofa near his chair, determined not to get depressed. "I'm having a cup of coffee," she said. "Can I pour you one?" The tray held two cups and saucers and a shiny black pot of freshly brewed coffee.

He pointed to a glass on the small table near his chair. "I'm working on a drink."

She poured the coffee. "I need to ask you something. People have mentioned a Violet to me. They seem to think I know about her, which I don't." She put the coffeepot down and looked up at him, her heart beating wildly. "Is there anything in particular you'd like me to say when they mention her to me?"

His face was impassive. "No."

"Everybody seems to know who she is. They're wondering whether you broke up or whether she's only in Europe temporarily and is coming back."

"The rumor mill will grind out gossip stories no matter what's said. My personal affairs are no one's business, wouldn't you agree?"

She sipped her coffee. "Of course. I'll just be pleasantly noninforming. I'm getting really good at that."

He nodded. "I've noticed."

She drank her coffee, while Ramsey went back to his drink and his papers. She'd found out exactly nothing, and she was too proud to ask him anything further. After all, his personal life was not her concern, as he had made abundantly clear. He might comfort her when she was crying, he might kiss her with real passion, but she was not to get too close to him. It was a bitter thought.

Ten minutes later they were on their way to the Ritz-Carlton for the reception. Samantha smiled, shook hands, Ramsey's arm around her. He was his attentive self, introducing her, smiling at her, not letting her out of his sight.

Tonight it was too much to take. No matter how hard she tried, she kept hearing his voice echoing in her head. "You don't need to get to know me, Samantha." His

arm around her became unbearable. He was deep in
conversation about the construction of a dam in
Venezuela when she took her chance and escaped. One
thing she had learned in the past few weeks was how to
mingle and circulate. It wasn't necessary to talk too
much. A few strategic questions and all you needed to
do was listen.

So she listened. There was a congressional aide who
seemed quite taken with her, but he was even more taken
with himself and was fully prepared to spend the evening
entertaining her with his utterly dull explanations of his
many important duties. She managed to get away, to be
drawn into conversation by an Arab oil sheikh who was
considerably more entertaining. Also more charming and
handsome.

She was laughing and having rather a good time, when
she felt an arm coming around her and found Ramsey
at her side.

He gave the sheikh a cool nod. "Would you excuse
us, please?" he said curtly, and let Samantha away.

"What's wrong?" she asked, piqued by his imperious
way of laying claim on her.

"Nothing. I just want you with me."

"I was enjoying talking to him," she said in a per-
verse attempt to annoy him.

"I'm sorry I had to break up your cozy tête-à-tête."
His tone of voice indicated that he wasn't sorry in the
least.

She gritted her teeth and let it ride.

Halfway through the evening she spotted Jeremy by
the buffet table. She hadn't known he would be at the
reception and she didn't actually talk to him until she
met him in the hotel foyer on her way back from the
ladies' room.

"So what are you doing here?" she asked, smiling.
"It's all oil sheikhs and shrimp potentates from the Far
East. Doing a piece on shrimp?"

He laughed. "No, on hotels and what they offer up
for sustenance at bashes like this."

"What a job!" she said.

"Never a dull moment. So, how is the old boy?"

"The old boy? Oh, Ramsey." She gave a casual shrug. "Talking business, as usual." She watched his gaze move from her face, taking in something past her shoulders. His smile faded.

"I'd better go. See you later, Samantha." He turned and was gone.

Surprised a little at his abrupt departure, she watched his retreating back, then shrugged. She turned to go in search of Ramsey, to find him only paces away, watching her, his face like granite, his eyes furious.

CHAPTER NINE

"WERE you just talking to Jeremy Kramer?" Ramsey demanded, his voice grim.

"I was, yes. Something wrong?"

"Stay away from him. He's no good."

Samantha laughed. "I can take care of myself."

"That's what you think."

Her mouth almost dropped open. "Ramsey, I can talk to him if I want to!"

"I want you to stay away from him!" He took her elbow. "End of discussion."

"Oh, no, it isn't!"

He gave her a warning look. "We'll discuss it later, then, but not now and not here. Now smile. I'm going to introduce you to the shrimp king of Malaysia. He's a personal friend, so be nice."

She gritted her teeth. "Don't tell me when to smile!"

He gave an exasperated sigh. "Samantha, don't make a scene."

She was ready to make one, right then and there. Who was he to tell her to whom she could or could not speak? But her good sense prevailed. Looking Ramsey squarely in the face, she produced a smile. Her heart wasn't in it and it lacked authenticity, she was sure, but a smile it was. "Of course not," she said nicely.

"That's better." He took her arm again and led her back into the reception room.

"Just so you know this discussion isn't over," she said on a low note.

"As you please."

And she had no intention of forgetting it, either. By the time they were back in his penthouse later that night, she'd built up enough steam inside for an explosion.

"I want to talk," she said as soon as Ramsey had closed the door behind them. She dropped her wrap and bag onto a chair. The place was very quiet; Mrs. Gregory had left hours ago.

"So talk," he said. He stood by the door, hands on his hips.

"You have no right to interfere in my private life," she said tightly. "There's nothing in our agreement to that effect."

"While you're with me through the holiday season," he said tightly, "it would be...indiscreet, and possibly dangerous, for you to be in Kramer's company at any time."

She rolled her eyes. "Now that makes it clear!"

He gave her a dark, compelling stare. "There are things I can't explain to you, and I would appreciate it if you'd take it on faith."

She clenched her hands. "No."

"I'm paying you eight thousand dollars," he said with grim determination.

She gritted her teeth. "You are not *paying me*. You're making a *donation* to ACTION—out of the goodness of your heart, to help people less fortunate than you. We have an agreement. It didn't say anywhere that I can't go out with other men, or talk to them or anything. If the timing doesn't conflict with your schedule of events, I see no harm..."

"Well, I do."

She squared her shoulders and looked him straight in the eyes. "It's simply not reasonable for you not to give me a better reason! I want to know what you have against him. He's a perfectly decent human being. He's a food writer who does articles for magazines. What's wrong with that?"

His eyes leaped with sudden anger and his body grew rigid with tension. Samantha stared at him, feeling the sudden silence quivering around her. What had she said to cause such an intense reaction?

He shouldered out of his jacket and tossed it on a chair. "So Jeremy's the man with whom you went to dinner on Tuesday night," he said coldly. It was a statement, not a question.

"Yes."

"And he told you he was *what*?"

"A free-lance food writer."

"Well, he's lying."

She felt her heart sink. "Oh, great!"

"Indeed." Ramsey loosened his tie and pulled it off. She watched him, thinking it seemed to be an oddly intimate thing to be watching, which was ridiculous. A tie was only a tie. Yet with his tie off, the top buttons of his shirt undone, he suddenly looked less... contained, more human.

"So what is he, if not a food writer?"

"Oh, he's a writer all right. He's a financial reporter. I'm in the middle of very sensitive negotiations. If he gets any whiff of it, we could be in big trouble."

Samantha raised her brows. "You mean to say he might want to get information out of me?" Damn you, Jeremy, she thought, you were using me.

"Exactly."

She laughed—she couldn't help it. Was this what he was getting all worked up about? Because she might give Jeremy information? "You've got to be kidding!"

"No," he bit out, "I'm damn well not kidding!"

She studied his face with growing apprehension. He was actually losing his control, and for no reason that made any sense to her at all. What could she possibly tell Jeremy that had any significance?

"I don't know anything about anything, Ramsey. What could I possibly tell him? You never tell me what you're doing. I know nothing about your business, you know that."

"I can't be careful enough."

"But that's crazy! He could put me on a medieval torture rack and get nothing out of me!"

His face was a rigid mask. "Samantha, I do not, and I repeat, *do not* want you to see or speak to him again while you're with me."

She gave a bitter laugh. "You mean to say that once it's January I'm free to tell him all your secrets?"

He glared at her, jaws clamped together. She'd never seen him so angry. Then, without a word, he turned on his heel and strode out of the room.

It was late when she awoke the next morning, and she was sure Ramsey had long ago left the apartment. She pulled on a robe and went in search of Mrs. Gregory and coffee, both of which she found in the kitchen.

As she sipped the potent Jamaican brew, she listened absently as Mrs. Gregory talked about her two sons, one of them almost a doctor, the other studying engineering at Cornell, their education being made possible by financial assistance from Ramsey.

"I don't know what we'd have done without him, you know. When my husband died..." She sighed. "We always hoped the boys would go to college and we saved every penny we could, but alone I couldn't do it." She flipped some pancakes onto Samantha's plate.

"Thank you." Samantha doused them liberally with maple syrup.

"He said it was one of his better investments," Mrs. Gregory went on. "He says investing in people is always better than investing in things or companies."

"Really?"

Mrs. Gregory nodded. "That's what he said."

Samantha ate her breakfast, digesting this bit of information. She thought of the orphanage on Saint Barlow that Alicia had told her about, and the children who came to Philadelphia for medical treatment. Ramsey had never told her about it, and she wondered what else he might be involved in. Investing in people. It was an interesting thought.

The limo took her back home and she spent the rest of the morning doing laundry and chopping wood.

Melissa came by in the afternoon on her way home from the shopping mall where she'd bought bags of Christmas gifts she wanted to show off. With parents, five brothers and sisters and a number of small nieces and nephews, she found it a major challenge to get it all done in time for Christmas. Samantha too was buying gifts for everyone, and she was looking forward to staying overnight at the big house at the edge of town on Christmas Eve and be part of the family.

"You have any chocolates left?" Melissa asked, after she had taken all the gifts out of the bags and spread them out for inspection.

"You didn't think I ate them all myself, did you?"

"You never know. How was the reception last night? Meet any interesting people?"

Samantha put the box of chocolates on the coffee table. "Listen to this. Jeremy Kramer was there, and when Ramsey saw me talking to him he had a fit." Samantha relayed the happenings of the night before.

"Very interesting," Melissa said, thoughtfully savoring another chocolate. "You know what it seems like to me? He's jealous."

"Jealous? Oh, come on, Melissa, you know better than that."

"Do you have a better explanation?"

"There's got to be one."

"Well, it certainly can't be the one he gave you, you know that. It's crazy to think you could give away Ramsey's secrets when he's never told you anything. Why would he make up something like that? It's ludicrous."

"His being jealous doesn't make sense either."

"Would it be so strange for him to fall in love with you?"

"He doesn't want to be involved right now. Besides, maybe he's only waiting for that Violet to come home. And if he's through with her he could find plenty of prospects more suitable than me." Samantha sighed and waved her hand. "Let's forget it for now."

After Melissa had left Samantha glanced at the clock. Simon would arrive in twenty minutes to take her back to the penthouse. One more evening with Ramsey, one more night alone in the pretty room in his apartment, one more night full of impossible dreams. Why should she put herself through this? He didn't want her, just her company until the season was over.

He enjoyed being with her. She made him feel good—that was what he had said. She was just the entertainment for the season. It was a bitter thought.

Stop moaning, she told herself. You agreed to his proposition. ACTION is going to get a large donation, and that's what this is all about. So lift up your chin, smile and do what you promised to do.

She took a deep breath and closed her eyes tightly.

If only she could get rid of that ache in her heart.

"I don't understand," she said several hours later. "This is the Kennedy Center."

Ramsey smiled. "So it is. Change of plans."

"You didn't tell me." Simon held the door open and she got out of the limo, gathering the heavy silk folds of her long skirt, so as not to get entangled in them.

"It's a surprise." He followed her out, put his arm around her and ushered her inside. The place was alive with people in evening clothes, glittery gowns, sparkling jewels, men in black evening suits and bow ties.

"What surprise?"

"The Columbia Ballet, performing *The Prince of the Pagodas*. Opening night, by invitation only."

A rush of excitement tingled through her body. "*The Prince of the Pagodas?* Really?" She could feel her face glow with enthusiasm. "Oh, Ramsey, that's great!"

He smiled, his eyes amused as he looked at her. "I'm glad you like it."

"I love the ballet." She glanced around. "Are we meeting other people? I mean, what social obligation is this?"

"It's just the two of us. No obligation. You told me you'd studied ballet for years, so I thought you might enjoy this."

Her face flushed warm. "Oh, Ramsey, I can't believe it! This is wonderful!"

And it was, every minute of the magical fairy tale. It trapped her into a web of delight, transporting her to a plane of magical happenings. She felt herself caught into a dream, a dream that didn't leave her even after they were back in the limousine. She could still hear the music, see the dazzling dancers, still feel the magic spell surrounding her.

She reached for Ramsey's hand. "Thank you so much. This was the best evening yet," she said, feeling herself flow over with happiness.

His hand felt warm. She relaxed her grip, but his fingers curled around hers, not letting go. She sighed and leaned back against the seat, smiling, still hearing in her head the lovely sounds.

"Why did you decide to take me to the ballet?" she asked once they were back in the penthouse.

"I wanted you to have a night out for yourself."

Warmth flooded her. She looked up at him, wanting to say something—something more than just a simple thank you.

"Thank you," she said. She reached up and put her arms around his neck and kissed him. It was done without conscious thought. It was what she needed to do on some deep instinctive level, to express what she felt this moment with more than simple words. The feelings of wonder and magic seemed to extend into the touching of their mouths, the dance of their tongues, the sense of delirium spreading through her. She leaned into him, molding herself to him, and the closeness felt right and good and like nothing she had ever experienced before. It was more than just bodies touching.

Until conscious thought returned and she realized the intimacy of the embrace was anything but innocent. She had revealed her feelings for him in a way that left no doubt, leaving herself exposed and defenseless. Her heart pounding, she tried to draw away, only to find his arms gently holding her back.

She stilled, her eyes locked with his. The silence thundered in her ears. She wanted to say something, but her tongue wouldn't move. There was no need for words. He would have no trouble interpreting her feelings from the way she had kissed him.

She was trembling. "I think," she said, trying to sound light and casual, "I was overdoing the gratitude."

"Am I complaining?"

"No, but then you're a gentleman."

His mouth quirked. "Believe me, I was quite enjoying it."

"Ramsey, I..." She swallowed the words. I know you don't want me to know you, she finished in her head. She saw the warm lights in his eyes, his mouth curving into a smile. She felt the gentle pressure of his hands on her bare back, then his mouth brushing her lips.

"I've been waiting for you, Samantha."

CHAPTER TEN

"YOU'VE been waiting for me?" Samantha couldn't think. It seemed that all she was aware of was her body, his kiss still lingering on her lips.

Ramsey drew her closer. "I made you a promise," he said against her ear, "and I don't break my promises, no matter how much I regret them."

"Promise? What...?"

"No sexual duties required—you made me put it in writing."

"Oh, yes." She drew in a steadying breath. "You just wanted me for company. Were you really expecting me to sleep with you?"

He laughed. "I'm not a saint, Samantha. The thought did occur to me, yes. But what choice did I have but to give you what you wanted in black-and-white on paper? You didn't know me and you certainly didn't trust me. And you certainly weren't after my money, or you wouldn't have asked for that condition."

She'd wanted to protect herself, but now everything had changed. Despite everything, she had fallen in love with him, with the hidden warmth in his smile, the silent hunger in his eyes. He dominated her thoughts and dreams, and she wanted more than anything to make love with the real man behind the glossy image of wealth and power.

"Samantha?" His tongue traced seductively across her lips. "Tell me what you want."

He knew what she wanted, there was no way he could not know. She had impulsively thrown her arms around him and allowed her feelings to take over and carry her away—feelings that had been trapped for too long, and needed to be expressed.

She did not now want to fight her feelings, and the delicious desire creeping through her body. Maybe she should. Maybe she should not love him, this man who kept so much of himself hidden beneath that cool, controlled exterior, this man who had hurt her with his words. Yet she did. There was no escaping that she loved him and wanted him.

"Samantha, say something." His voice was low and rough. "I can't stand here like this much longer. Tell me..." His mouth closed over hers, hot and demanding, his arms pressing her against him. "Tell me...tell me...you want me."

"I want you," she whispered, clinging to him, her knees trembling, her bones weakening. "Only... I'm...I'm not prepared. I mean..."

A low, soft moan came from deep in his throat. "I'll take care of it. Don't worry about it." Then his mouth again, full of passion and urgency, and her own meeting his in equal fervor. She felt stunned by the intensity, the desperate hunger of the kiss. Her head was swimming and she no longer felt the floor beneath her feet.

He released her mouth suddenly, drawing in a ragged breath. He drew back a little so he could see her face, his eyes locking with hers.

"I've never wanted anyone as much as I want you," he said huskily. "You're lovely and warm and wonderful, and I want to make love to you." He swooped her up into his arms and carried her from the room, the silk of her long gown swishing sensuously against her. His bedroom was in darkness. He set her down on the floor and steadied her, reaching out with one hand to switch on a small lamp. The room came alive with a soft glow. He straightened and smiled into her eyes, weaving his hands through her hair, working it loose until it fell heavily around her bare shoulders. He trailed a finger across her lips, smiling a little.

"You drive me crazy with that laughing mouth of yours, you know that?" he said softly. "And those golden eyes, full of the devil. I go crazy thinking of what you'll look like naked in my arms, what I'll see in your eyes when I make love to you." He touched his mouth to her cheek, his tongue making a damp trail down her jaw and chin and neck, his hands stroking her bare shoulders, then sliding around to her back.

He unzipped her dress and slowly slipped the strapless bodice down, exposing her breasts. He stood back and looked at her. She shivered a little, pinpricks of electricity tingling through her. He cupped her breasts in his warm hands, letting their weight rest in his palms. Bending his head, he kissed one, then the other, his lips feather light and satiny warm on her skin. He lifted his face to look at her and she felt heat radiating through her. It was hard to breathe. It was hard to stand there with her legs trembling and her head dizzy with feverish sensations.

The dress rustled to the floor, drifting into a shapeless mound of shimmering fabric, leaving her with only her silky tights and long half-slip, of which he divested her in swift, expert movements.

"Samantha..." he whispered, his gaze caressing her with velvet fire, setting her aglow—her skin, her blood. Her breathing came in shallow little gasps and her pulse was racing. In the soft glow, his face was different, the sharp angles and lines smoother, his eyes darker.

Samantha closed her eyes, trembling with need. She wanted him naked too, to touch him, feel his bare skin against hers. "Ramsey," she whispered, for no other reason but to say his name. Reaching out, she unbuttoned his shirt, pulling it out of the waistband of his pants and slipping it off his shoulders. She saw the rise and fall of his chest, a tanned chest with a light mat of dark hair. Wrapping her arms around him, steadying herself, she nestled her face against the warmth of his chest, feeling the roughness of his hair tickling her cheek. The clean, warm scent of him, so very male and intoxicating, filled her being.

"I want to lie down," she whispered. He lifted her up and put her down on the big bed. He stood and un-

buckled his belt and threw off the rest of his clothes,
unselfconscious about his nakedness and arousal.

She looked at him, at the male beauty of shape and
muscle and color, and she thought she would burst into
flame. He lay down beside her. His fingers, light and
caressing, began to move with tantalizing delicacy across
her body. She floated away on a warm cloud, away from
the reality of floors and walls and furniture, away from
warning bells and realism and prices to pay and sacrifices to make.

A storm of sensations gathered inside her. She wanted
to give in to the madness, the sheer wonder of the
pleasure of her body. She was aware of all caution, all
self-consciousness dissolving, leaving her feeling rich with
feeling, rich with power. She turned on her side, reaching
toward him, kissing his mouth, wanting to give him what
he was giving her.

She was wild and free, and she laughed softly, de-
lightedly, as she began to stroke him in turn, exploring
the texture and contours of his body, kissing him, her
tongue tasting his skin, trailing damp circles on his
stomach. She felt him tremble, heard his shallow
breathing.

She felt herself slipping into that magic world of
loving, existing outside time and place and thought, a
world where nothing mattered but the pleasure of loving
and the meeting of the spirit.

On and on, until he gave a low tortured groan and
turned, moving over her, his body melding with hers in
ancient ritual. All was pure, primitive pleasure, old as
the world. Passion and fire, a sweet, aching rapture filled
her consciousness. Her fingers curled into the damp
tangle of his hair.

"Oh," she whispered, "oh, Ramsey." And then it was
there, pulsing through her, a primal, timeless, eternal
force, matching his in perfect harmony.

"I was right," he said, smiling down at her. "All that
lovely, unbridled passion, it's all there." With a gentle

finger he traced the contours of her mouth. "You're the most loving, generous person I know, Samantha, in and out of bed."

"It's a real sacrifice, believe me." She offered him a devilish smile. "Just think of what I got out of it."

He laughed softly, lowering his face to her breasts, brushing his lips across her skin.

"Talk about being generous," she said. "You give hundreds of thousands of dollars away—for the medical treatment of the orphanage children from Saint Barlow, and the education of Mrs. Gregory's sons, and now ACTION. And I imagine there's plenty more that I don't know about." She felt her heart race, yet she couldn't help saying what she had just said.

Ramsey raised his face and frowned. "How do you know all that?"

"Oh, come on, Ramsey. People talk."

He shrugged. "Well, it's only money."

"That's easy to say when you've got plenty. But to the people you're giving it to it means everything. You're making your money count for something, and nobody forces you to give it away."

He rolled over on his back, drawing her on top of him. "Can we change the subject?" he asked.

She smiled and kissed his chin. "Sure. Well, let's see, what can we talk about?" She laced her fingers through the dark thickness of his hair. "Tell me, what did you like most about your life when you were little?"

"Going fishing with my father, just the two of us. It made me feel very important." He gave a smile that had sadness in its depths. His hands were stroking her bare back, absently, gently.

"Did you go often?"

"No, but now and then, until my parents divorced. I hardly saw him after that, and when I did he was always busy."

"You must have felt abandoned," she said.

His face closed up. The light went out of his eyes, and he shrugged. "That's life."

She sensed his withdrawal, like hearing a door close. But perhaps it was not withdrawal from her. Perhaps he withdrew from himself, from the part of himself that had been wounded as a small boy.

"What about your mother? Did you live with her?"

He laughed, but it held no humor. "She sent me to boarding school. She was also very busy—especially with acquiring new husbands."

It didn't take a lot of imagination to picture his childhood. All material comforts and little love. How very different from her own life.

Samantha lowered her face and nibbled his ear. "What did you want most as a kid?" she asked casually. When he didn't answer immediately, she lifted her face and met his eyes.

His mouth curved in a wry smile. "A normal family, with two brothers, a dog, and my own airplane."

"No sisters?"

"Are you kidding?" There was humor in his voice now. "Girls were dumb. They played with dolls and cried when you pushed them."

"Oh, of course—how *dumb* of me to forget. Is that why you've never married? Because girls are dumb and they cry when you push them?"

He laughed. "I don't see myself in a long-term relationship, as a husband and father. I never did. Of all the many risks I take, that one is not for me."

There were a thousand questions, but she was afraid if she pushed too much he'd withdraw from her again, and she didn't want to take that chance.

He turned her over on her back again and put his face against her breasts. "Spend Christmas with me," he said, his voice muffled.

She looked down on his dark head, speechless.

He lifted his face to look at her. "We'll reserve Christmas dinner at the Willard. I'll get some French movies and we can watch them in front of the fire, and you can tell me about life in Aurora and the kids in your class."

"But I'm going to have Christmas with Melissa's family."

"Tell them you've made other plans."

She was silent, thinking about the big house full of people, most of whom she'd known since she was five. She thought of the attic room she'd share with Melissa and an assortment of her tiny nieces. She thought of all the warmth and joy and laughter of Christmas at Melissa's family's house.

She thought of Ramsey taking off to some tropical island to escape Christmas. Of his mother, whose Christmas party was a publicity event at a Hawaiian beach.

He sat up straight, raking both hands through his hair. "Sorry," he said then, "that wasn't fair. Forget I said anything." He leaped out of bed. "Let me see if I can manage to work the coffeemaker and find some breakfast." He pulled on his robe.

Samantha threw off the covers. "I'll help."

"Don't trust me by myself in the kitchen?"

She laughed. "Not for a minute."

It was Sunday and Mrs. Gregory was not in. They fried eggs and ham and made toast. It seemed homey and intimate to sit here with Ramsey eating breakfast, leafing through the Sunday paper, talking about the latest news and the stories in the paper.

This was what she wanted, not the fancy, glittering life-style they shared on their nights out. She wanted a man to share the simple things of life with. A man to belong with.

He put the paper down. "More coffee?"

"Please."

She watched him as he filled the cups. "I'd like to spend Christmas with you," she said.

He looked up, surprised. "I shouldn't have asked."

"But you did."

He handed her the cup. "You have plans, Samantha."

"Do you *want* us to spend Christmas together?"

He sat down. "I do, but what do you want?" His eyes held hers and she felt her heart fluttering nervously.

"I'd like to be with you," she told him.

He didn't smile. "Sure?"

"Yes."

"Then let's do it."

"There's one condition. I won't go to any hotel for Christmas dinner in public. I'll cook it and we can have it right here."

"Why go to the trouble? It isn't necessary."

"Of course it is! It isn't right otherwise. Maybe we'll have duck—a turkey is a lot for just two people. Or would you like to invite some friends?"

"I'm sure they've all made other plans by now, and I'd prefer to be alone with you."

"All right, then." She straightened, her mind racing, "I'll get to it."

A smile curved his mouth. "You've got stars in your eyes."

"Oh." She laughed. "Well, it's Christmas in just a few days. Why not?"

"Why not indeed?"

On Tuesday night, ACTION volunteers again assembled food boxes for the needy families in the area. Samantha had been working ever since school came out, organizing the volunteers and sorting the cans and boxes. She was tired. Today had been the last school day before the holidays, and the children had been restless and excited.

Last night Jeremy had called, telling her he was leaving suddenly for a new assignment in Geneva and asking if he could please see her once more before the plane would carry him away from her many charms.

"I don't think so," she'd said coolly. "I have this inconvenient little rule. I don't go out with crooks and swindlers."

"Ouch," he said. "You're being awfully harsh, Samantha. Just remember, all's fair in love and war."

"Goodbye, Jeremy." She'd hung up.

Someone tapped her on the shoulder. "We've got twelve bags of food," the man said. "Sorry we're late. Where would you like us to put them?"

Samantha pointed. "Over there. Thank you so much."

Things were going well for the moment. She could take a break and sit for a minute. Grabbing a bread roll and a cup of coffee, she sat down and surveyed the hustle and bustle in the room for anything she might have missed.

And she had indeed missed something.

Ramsey was standing in line with a box. There was no mistaking him for anyone else, even though he was wearing jeans and a sweater. Her heart made a crazy somersault and warmth rushed through her. She hadn't seen him since Sunday, the day after they'd made love. He'd flown to London that afternoon and she hadn't expected to see him again until tomorrow, when she was due to move into the apartment until the end of the year.

He had not been out of her thoughts. Thinking of making a Christmas for the two of them filled her with excitement, an emotion that was not shared by Melissa.

"I'm not being selfish about it, Sam. I'm sorry you won't be with us, but what bothers me is—"

"I know what bothers you, Melissa. I appreciate your concern, but this is the way I want it. I don't know what will happen, I only know I can't stop it. I want to be with him." Samantha had smiled brightly. "I suppose if I want to ruin my life I've got the right to do it."

I can't stop it I can't stop it I can't stop it. The words had popped up in her head at the oddest moments. She felt helpless against that mysterious force that was drawing her to Ramsey. Love, she thought. I love him. One day I'll have to pay, but I can't help myself.

She watched him now, putting food into a box. Quickly putting down her cup, she came to her feet and hurried over to him.

"Well, hello there," she said, feeling a happy grin spread out over her face.

He looked up, a can of tuna fish in his hand. "Hello, Samantha." His eyes were laughing.

"I can't believe what I'm seeing," she said. "Why are you here?"

"I thought you might need some help."

She laughed. "You were in London the last two days. You must have tons of work to do."

"I'm the boss. I decide." He moved on to the next table.

She squeezed his arm. "Thank you. Oh, by the way, Jeremy Kramer called last night. He said he has a new assignment in Geneva."

"Is that right?" His tone was even.

"You wouldn't have anything to do with that, would you?"

He met her eyes. "I won't try to insult your intelligence."

"I appreciate that. Why did you do it?"

"To get him out of the way, of course." He carried his box to the next table. "Two adults, one child, please," he said to the volunteer manning the table.

Samantha retreated. Asking more questions would not be fruitful. Also not necessary. Melissa had been right—Ramsey was jealous. Samantha smiled inwardly.

Ramsey stayed and worked till the job was done and all the volunteers had left, then he followed her little red Toyota home in the limousine.

Once inside he took her in his arms and kissed her. "This was one hell of a couple of days," he said. "I just got back late this afternoon."

"You must be exhausted." Over his shoulder she glanced at the clock. "It's almost two in the morning in London." And still he had come to the school to help. Or to see her. Or both.

"I'm fine," he said.

She shivered suddenly. "It's cold in here. Let me rake up the fire." She poked at the half-burned logs in the stove and they obediently began to flame up. She added a couple of fresh logs and put the screen in front, leaving the doors open.

"Everybody's talking about the limo that comes and picks me up all the time," she said, straightening.

"What are they saying?"

She laughed. "Wild stories, but no one knows the truth, except Melissa and Alicia."

"And tomorrow you're going to disappear until the first of the year. Then they'll really have something to talk about."

"I've told everybody I'm out of town visiting friends." She pointed at her suitcase, ready for the move to his penthouse. "I'm all ready."

"You could come with me now, if you like," he said.

She'd expected Simon to come and get her in the morning, but what difference would it make? She took his hand, an idea forming in her head.

"Or you could stay with me tonight," she suggested.

It was, in many ways, a strange thought. It didn't fit the pattern of their relationship, which conducted itself in the luxury of Ramsey's penthouse apartment and the bright lights of Washington's elegant social life. The few times he had come to her house, she had been aware of how out of place he seemed. She wondered now, as she spoke the words, what his reaction would be.

He bent his face to hers, his mouth near her ear.

"I've been wanting to try out that brass bed of yours," he told her.

"How did you know I have one?"

"I saw it that Sunday afternoon when I found you asleep on the couch. I came in through the back door, remember? Your bedroom door was open." His mouth moved to hers, his lips sliding sensuously across hers. "It's a very cozy, inviting bed," he murmured. The moist tip of his tongue caressed her lips. Then, hungrily, he claimed her mouth fully. He made an inarticulate sound, drawing her more closely against the length of his body.

She yielded to him, her mouth inviting him, her body flooding with warm, dizzy excitement. The feel of him,

the scent of him filled her senses. He made her body
sing with a single touch, a magic power no one else had
ever had over her.

His hands slipped under her sweater, sliding over her
bare back, then to the front where they cupped her
breasts. "I want you," he muttered. "I want you now,
Samantha."

"All right," she whispered. "Let's try out my brass
bed."

His loving was fierce and passionate, seducing her
body into a wildness of her own. She sensed in his love-
making an odd quality of desperation, and somewhere
in the dark recess of her mind she wondered what ghosts
he was fighting. But conscious thought melted away with
the heat of his touch, the fire of his need. There was
nothing but the delicious intoxication of her senses, the
primitive abandon of her body, and, in the end, the blind
rapture of release.

It took a long time to drift back to earth, and she lay
in his arms, silent and sated, knowing she loved him.

Early the next morning the limousine drove them back
to Washington, and while Ramsey was at the office
Samantha went out and bought a real Christmas tree,
lights and trimmings, and lots of candles. With Mrs.
Gregory's help, she decorated the apartment and went
shopping for Christmas dinner food.

"He never wanted me to do anything," Mrs. Gregory
said as they unloaded the groceries in the kitchen. "Told
me not to bother. Can you imagine? For Christmas! I
don't think he cared for Christmas much. He'd go off
to some island in the Caribbean to go sailing." She
looked indignant. "I'm glad you managed to talk some
sense into him."

The next day was Christmas Eve, and in the morning
Samantha was in the kitchen baking cranberry bread.
Mrs. Gregory and the daily maid had been given three
days off, Samantha having insisted she was perfectly

capable of taking care of things for a few days on her own.

She plugged the mixer into the outlet and took out a couple of mixing bowls. Tomorrow was Christmas. Then one more week and the agreement would be over. She felt her heart contract in sudden fear. What would happen then? Would it simply end? Would Ramsey give her the check and say, "Thank you, Samantha. I enjoyed knowing you." Her hand shook as she deposited the mixing bowls on the counter.

Don't think about it, she told herself. Enjoy the time you have. Who knows? Maybe a miracle will happen. After all, this is Christmas and it's magic time.

She had brought some Christmas tapes with her, and she went into the living room and put one of them into the stereo system. A moment later, cheerful music danced into the air.

Samantha went back into the kitchen and set to work. It was wonderful to work in such a well-designed kitchen. All the ingredients were spread out, the flour and honey, the nuts and cranberries. She measured ingredients, consulting the recipe, broke eggs, and mixed the batter with a wooden spoon.

She was singing along with the music at the top of her voice when suddenly something caught her awareness— movement, a prickling at the back of her neck. The song ended, as did the tape, and the ensuing stillness had an odd, threatening quality. Samantha turned her head.

A woman was standing in the entry to the kitchen. A tall redhead with frigid gray eyes, a fur coat draped over one arm.

Samantha stood stock still and stared. She was magnificent—a glamour model from *Vogue* magazine, a film star, an ice princess from Europe.

Magnificent. And furious.

"Who the hell are you?" the woman demanded.

CHAPTER ELEVEN

SAMANTHA wetted her lips and tried to compose herself, thoughts and questions racing through her head. Who was this woman? How had she got in?

"I asked you a question," the woman said. "Who the hell are you?"

Don't let her get to you. You've learned how to deal with types like her in the last few weeks. Go for it!

Samantha widened her eyes and gave the woman a bright, surprised smile. "Me?" She gestured around the kitchen, the flour, the cake pans. "I'm the maid, ma'am," she said, injecting her voice with a touch of Southern twang.

The cold gray eyes narrowed suspiciously. "Where's Mrs. Gregory?"

"She's off for the holidays. I'm filling in temporarily," Samantha said cheerfully.

"Where's Mr. MacMillan?"

"Ramsey is out shopping, ma'am," she said primly. She watched the face react to her use of Ramsey's first name. She was not disappointed; the lady didn't like it one bit. Samantha smiled sweetly and stirred the batter with a wooden spoon.

"When will he be back?"

"I'm afraid I have no idea. It could be hours. Would you like to wait? I could make you a cup of coffee, or a sandwich perhaps?"

There was an ominous silence. "I think," the woman said slowly, "I'll have a shower and change. Then you can make me a cup of coffee." She turned on her high heels and marched down the hall in the direction of the bedrooms.

Samantha realized she'd forgotten to breathe. She took in a gulp of air. Her heart was racing.

Be calm now, she admonished herself. This may mean nothing. Perhaps she's a cousin, dropping in unexpectedly to spend the holidays with poor lonely Ramsey.

Fat chance. She swallowed, automatically adding the cranberries and walnuts to the batter and stirring it. The crimson berries drowned in the muddy batter. It looked quite disgusting, actually, but it would be delicious once it was baked—sweet with honey, tart with berries, rich with walnuts. Oh, God, who was this woman? She pressed her eyes closed. Don't let this get to you. Don't think. Don't feel. Later she would think.

"What the hell is this?" The voice rang shrilly in the silence, and Samantha opened her eyes.

The woman was standing in the doorway, holding Samantha's robe with two fingers as if she thought it might be contaminated.

"It's a robe, ma'am," she said.

"I *know* what it is. Whose is it?"

Samantha looked straight at her, pausing meaningfully. "You asked *what*, not *whose*." Damn that woman, damn her tone. She poured the batter into the pans.

"I'd like to know what's going on here," the woman demanded, her voice full of barely controlled rage. "Who put up that tree? The candles? All those decorations?"

Samantha looked up. "I did."

"How cozy!" She looked Samantha up and down. "Such domesticity—how touching. And I expect this thing is yours as well?"

"Yes, it is."

"I'll be damned. The bastard. I go out of the country for a couple of months and the next thing I know he's fooling around with some floozy."

Samantha could feel herself grow cold with fury. "And who can blame him?" she said.

For a moment she thought the woman was going to jump at her. "If you think for a moment you've got something going here, you're sadly mistaken!"

"Oh, I'm not mistaken. I *know* what I've got going."

The woman gave a mocking little laugh. "You're not going to get anything out of him, you know. He's a shrewd bastard, and believe me, I know."

Samantha let a faint, secretive smile play around her lips. "I've already got something out of him."

"Oh, is that right? And what might that be?"

She widened her smile. "It's a matter of the highest confidence, so I'm not at liberty to divulge it."

"Well, well, she's semiarticulate!"

"I can write too," said Samantha sweetly, "and type." She opened the oven door and placed the two loaf pans inside. She straightened and began to clear away the baking things, grateful to have something to keep her hands busy so she wouldn't stand there and tremble like a fool.

A fool was what she was. A romantic fool who trusted too easily, who gave of herself too easily. What had she expected? Of course there were women in Ramsey's life. And one of them was standing here in the flesh in her designer clothes and boots, claiming her territory.

Well, she could have it. In about an hour when the cranberry nut loaves were finished. No sense in wasting good food. She wiped the counter.

"I want you out of here," the woman said, her voice low and furious.

Samantha went on wiping. Then again, why should she leave? Because this redhaired witch was telling her to? It might be interesting to see what Ramsey would say or do when he came home and found her here. Clearly he had not been expecting her.

No, she wasn't going to play games. She'd made a mistake. She was smart enough to recognize it for what it was, and the best thing to do was to bow out gracefully. It was clear enough that he did not need her services any longer; Miss what's-her-name could handle it perfectly well.

"I want you out now," the woman snapped.

Samantha smiled. "Of course—no problem. If I'm not needed any longer I'll be glad to go. Let me just show you a couple of things." She opened the refrigerator. One more act to finish off the performance. Just to see how the lady would react. "The duck is in here," she went on. "I made cranberry relish and applesauce this morning, and they're in these covered dishes on this shelf. The stuffing isn't made up yet, but the ingredients are on the shelf in the pantry. Would you like me to leave the recipe for you?"

The woman stared at her speechlessly.

"You do cook, don't you?" Samantha asked, still holding the open refrigerator door.

"Are you suggesting I cook Christmas dinner?"

Samantha shrugged. "I was. We were staying home."

The woman advanced into the kitchen and grabbed the refrigerator door and slammed it shut. "To hell with that duck! If he wants to stay home, he'll do his own cooking."

"He might not know how to stuff a duck. He may need your help." Samantha wiped her hands on the towel. "Anyway, let me pack and I'll be out of here." She smiled brightly. "Oh, yes, the cranberry bread. The timer will go off in about fifty minutes. Check to see that it's done—the toothpicks are here." She moved past the woman into the hall, to her bedroom. Closing the door behind her, she let out a long breath. She was shaking all over. Acting was a lot harder than it looked.

It didn't take long to pack the few things she'd brought from home. She called a taxi and took her suitcase out to the front door. The woman was sitting on the couch in a long silk robe, smoking a cigarette, a drink in her hand. It looked like a double whisky straight up. It was eleven in the morning.

"Please tell Ramsey that in the circumstances I still expect the check by the end of the month," Samantha told her.

The woman's eyes widened. "What's that supposed to mean?"

"I'm afraid I can't explain. Just pass the message."

The woman jerked upright. "Is he *paying* you?"

"Not exactly, no."

"How exactly, then?"

"Why don't you ask Ramsey?"

"Oh, I will, don't worry."

Samantha opened the door. With her hand on the knob, she paused. "You're Violet, aren't you?"

The frigid eyes gave her a steely stare. "Yes."

Samantha nodded. "I thought so—I've heard about you. Ramsey has my condolences." She opened the door wider and smiled. "I'll be off now. Have a merry Christmas." She walked out and closed the door behind her and pressed the elevator button. The apartment door flung open before it arrived.

"You little bitch!" The woman's face was flushed. "Who the hell do you think you are?"

The elevator doors slid open. Samantha stepped in and faced the woman. "Just a temporary replacement, that's all." The doors closed and the elevator began its descent, along with Samantha's heart.

Don't think. Don't feel. Just go through the motions. She got off the elevator, moved through the apartment lobby, waved at the doorman, stepped outside.

It was a miserable day, cold and wet and windy, as if the world itself was in agreement with her mood. She took a taxi to the subway, contemplating the endless string of public and private vehicles that it would take to get her home to Aurora. To hell with it, she'd take a taxi all the way. Ramsey could foot the bill. After all, she was here because he had wanted her here. All she wanted now was to get home fast. Get safely inside her own small house, shut the door behind her and forget what had happened.

She leaned forward and spoke to the driver, who was more than willing to take on a long drive out of town and a big fare.

Outside the world was gray and watery, and Samantha looked at the people scuttling through the streets, heads bent against the rain and wind. Cars splashed through the puddles, spraying pedestrians and soaking their clothes. People everywhere carried shopping bags full of presents.

Tomorrow was Christmas Day.

Christmas. She had looked forward to it, planning their dinner. She'd let herself get wrapped up in this dream of romance and cozy togetherness—a Christmas tree, presents, a dinner. As if they were a couple. But they were not a couple. They could never be. In her saner moments she knew this. It was only when her romantic self took over that all reality bit the dust. In those times she spun a fairy tale of love and longing, of hope—a silly, unrealistic hope.

She watched the people hurrying through the streets. She'd never before felt so utterly lonely.

The house, when she arrived, was cold and clammy. She put paper and kindling in the stove and added some logs, then lit the paper. She watched the flames curl the paper and reach for the kindling. It began to crackle and smoke, then the draft sucked it up into the chimney and the fire began to roar. She put the screen on and left the doors open to get more of its warmth. Now a cup of hot cocoa to comfort her. She came to her feet and went into the kitchen. It was early afternoon, Christmas Eve. There was still time to go over to Melissa's. She'd call them in a little while and tell them what had happened. They'd welcome her with open arms. She wasn't alone at Christmas. She had a place to go. Why was she feeling sorry for herself?

With the hot cocoa in her hands she sat in front of the fire and watched the flames. Sitting here contemplating the state of affairs wasn't really a good idea. She'd better keep busy and think of something else. Bake a pie, go to the homeless shelter and read Christmas stories to the kids. Yet her body refused to move, as if some stupor had taken hold of her and all she could do was sit here and think of Ramsey.

"You make me feel good...you make me laugh."
'There's no need for you to get to know me, Samantha."

"There's no need for you to get to know me,
Samantha."

The loud knock on the door jarred her from her
stupor. She put the cup down and went to answer the
door.

Ramsey. She stared at him, her heart racing wildly in
her chest. "What are you doing here?" she managed at
last.

"I've come to take you back." He moved past her
into the house without waiting for her invitation.

She closed the door and faced him. "I don't understand."

"What's there to understand? You agreed to spend
Christmas with me. Not to mention the fact that we're
going out to dinner tonight at the Clarences'."

Her body grew tense. "I was told to leave."

"Not by me, you weren't."

"Your lady friend came home," she said. "It seemed
to me she could take care of your needs quite
adequately."

"She can't cook worth a damn." Humor sparked
briefly in his eyes.

"Well, yes, that is a problem," Samantha said caus-
tically, not finding the strength for humor. "So take her
out for dinner."

Ramsey made an impatient gesture. "I'm sorry this
happened. I wasn't expecting her. I didn't even know
she was back from Europe."

"Oh, heck."

"Temporary replacement"—her own words. How true
it was. He'd needed someone while Violet was gone. He
hadn't broken up with her at all. It was just what
everybody had thought.

His jaw grew rigid. "For God's sake, Samantha! I'm
not going to stand here and argue with you!" He advanced toward her, reaching out to her, but she moved

away from him. She didn't want him to touch her. Not ever again.

He jammed his hands into his pockets and held her gaze. "I want you to come back and have Christmas with me."

She gave an exasperated sigh. "Drop the gentleman act, will you? I know how important it is to you to keep your promises and agreements, but don't worry, I'll let you off the hook."

"I'm not on any hook. You're coming back with me!"

"Somehow I don't think your lady friend would appreciate that."

"Her name is Violet, and I don't give a damn about what she appreciates or not. I kicked her out."

"The day before Christmas? Not very charitable of you."

"Dammit, Samantha! She doesn't live with me and never did."

"Well, she certainly wanted me to think she did," she retorted.

"I don't doubt it for a moment—she's an expert manipulator. But she has no claims on me whatsoever, and she had no right to interfere in my life and no right to ship you out. She presumed way too much. I've dealt with her now, and you can be assured she won't bother you again."

Was she supposed to be relieved? She crossed her arms in front of her breast and said nothing.

"We have an agreement," he said when she remained silent.

"That's correct." An agreement that had nothing to do with her heart, with loving, with emotional commitment. Samantha felt her heart harden. She came to her feet. She wasn't going to act the betrayed woman. Ramsey hadn't betrayed her, because he had never promised her anything. She should be careful not to forget that. This was a business relationship.

Sure, sure, her little inner voice said.

She straightened her sweater over her hips. "All right, if that's what you want, I'll come back with you."

Was there relief in his eyes? She wasn't sure.

She reached for her coat. Her suitcase was still standing by the door where she had dropped it.

He glanced at the Christmas tree in the corner of the room and the wrapped gifts heaped under it.

"Are all these yours?" he asked.

"Yes. From my friends and Melissa's family. Melissa has a key. She brought them over after I left with you on Saturday. She called me." Samantha had brought only her gifts from Paul and Lee Ann and the girls with her to the apartment.

"Why didn't you have Simon pick them up so you could put them under the tree at my apartment?" he asked.

She shrugged. "I hadn't thought of it."

It was a lie. She had thought of it, but rejected it. How would it look if she piled all her gifts under his tree and all he had under it was the one from her and a few others? She'd asked him to put his presents under the tree, and four or five was all he'd put under it. It had surprised her. After all, didn't rich people give and receive lots of gifts? But there wasn't a discreet way of asking about his lack of presents, so she hadn't.

His eyes met hers and she looked away. He took a step closer and lifted her chin, a smile curving his lips. "You're a bad liar, Samantha. You were feeling sorry for me."

She widened her eyes. "Why would I feel sorry for you? That's crazy."

His mouth twitched. "You feel sorry for everybody."

"That's not true!"

"All the poor, disadvantaged, downtrodden, hungry, homeless people in the world."

She sighed. "Okay, all right. But so do a lot of others."

"So why do you feel sorry for me? I don't exactly fit any of the categories."

How was she going to answer that?

"Tell me," he insisted.

"You seem . . . very alone."

"How can you say that?" he asked lightly. "After I've taken you to all these places and introduced you to so many people."

"I don't think any of them are really your friends. I mean—" Samantha bit her lip "—you don't seem very close to anybody."

He shook his head slowly, holding her gaze. "There's no need to feel sorry for me, Samantha. Whatever loneliness I'm suffering from is self-inflicted. It's part of my life, my life-style." He gave a crooked smile. "And, to set your heart at ease, I did receive more gifts than the ones under the tree. They're at my office and I didn't feel like bringing them home. It's all the usual stuff I get every year—cases of cognac, cans of caviar, silk ties, the works." His gaze settled back on Samantha's presents under the tree.

"I want you to take them." He began to scoop up the packages in his arms. "Open the door."

She did as he ordered and he strode out to the limo. Simon hurried to his aid, opening the door so Ramsey could deposit the packages inside, then going into the house for the rest of them and her suitcase. Moments later they were on their way back to Washington.

"Would you care for a cup of coffee?" he asked, and Samantha shook her head.

"No, thank you."

He covered her hand with his. "I'm sorry this happened, Samantha."

She slipped her hand away from under his. "It's all right." She should be glad she was still spending Christmas with him, yet some of the shine had worn off. He had sent Violet away, yet the experience had marred the gloss of her happiness.

It had all seemed so simple in the beginning. All she had to do was accompany him to various functions and events. Then her heart had become involved, making everything more complicated. She glanced down at her hands in her lap, her eyes blurring.

If only he loved her.

Dinner at the Clarence house was a huge, formal affair with the usual razzle-dazzle of famous people. Photographers lay in ambush outside the door. Flashbulbs exploded in the dark. Reporters shouted, throwing up questions like helium balloons. They faded in the night and no one seemed to answer them.

A night of food, people, glitter, talk—too much talk. Everybody had something to say. Everybody wanted to be heard. During predinner cocktails, Samantha and Ramsey found themselves with a handsome scientist who talked enthusiastically about his trip to the Amazon. Samantha was enthralled with his stories, and, as the conversation went on, he became obviously enthralled with her. The only one not enthralled was Ramsey, who decided it was time to mingle.

"I liked talking to him," she said, annoyed. "You're always dragging me away when I'm talking to any male under forty." Not to mention what he had done in the case of Jeremy.

"You're imagining things," he said. "Come along now."

By the time they came back to the penthouse, she was exhausted from making small talk and her jaws ached from smiling.

"It's been a long day," she said lightly. "I'm off to bed."

"What's wrong?" He advanced toward her, but didn't touch her, much to her relief.

"Nothing. I'm just tired." She took a step backward, creating more space between them. "Good night."

"Samantha." He reached out and drew her to him, wrapping his arms tightly around her. "Please, don't do this, Samantha."

"Do what?" she asked.

"You know what. Don't turn away from me." He kissed her, sliding his lips gently across hers. "I want us to be together tonight. I want to hold you, make love to you."

She moved her face away from him, standing rigidly in his embrace. "Well...I don't...I can't."

"Why not?"

She felt tears burn behind her eyes. "Because I don't feel right about it! I'm sorry I ever started this in the first place!"

"Why?"

"Because...because...I feel *used*!" Tears were dripping down. "I'm just a temporary convenience for you. Oh, I don't blame you—it's my own fault. I'm stupid and naive, and it's time I grew up!" She struggled against his hold and he let his arms drop away. She tried to see his face, but tears blurred her vision.

"I'm not using you," he said on a low note. "I wanted you, yes, but you wanted me too. I didn't take advantage of you, Samantha. It was a mutual decision."

"Well, I made the wrong decision!" She turned and fled to her bedroom.

She lay in bed wondering what it was she had expected.

Ramsey owed her nothing. She had no right to make demands, no right to assume he felt about her the way she felt about him.

He wanted her. And what did that mean? She was not naive, so why was she acting like it?

Love and commitment had been given freely. She loved him, and more than anything in the world she longed for him to love her back. In the last few days it had seemed easy to believe that he did, but it was only because she had wanted to believe it, because she wanted so much for it to be true.

Despite all the blessings of her life, there was this aching need, this hollow spot in her heart that needed filling up. If only her heart hadn't very inconveniently decided that Ramsey was the man for the job.

What was she expecting, anyway? A proposal of marriage? Had she lost her mind completely? Ramsey wasn't the marrying kind, and he'd never made her believe otherwise.

Maybe he needed time. Maybe in time he would learn to change his ideas about love and commitment. Wasn't it at least worth a risk? In life sometimes you had to take a leap of faith.

If only she weren't so frightened.

She climbed out of bed and pulled on her robe.

She found him in the living room, sitting in the dark, with only the fire going.

Bare-footed, she moved across the soft rug to where he was sitting on the couch. She knelt by his side.

"Ramsey?"

He turned his head to face her. "Yes?"

"Why are you not in bed?"

"I couldn't sleep."

"I couldn't either."

Silence. She watched the flickering flames that threw strange shadows into the darkness of the room.

"I'm sorry we had an argument," she said at last.

"Yes."

"I was upset because of Violet. I felt . . . humiliated."

"I know. I know how she can be." His hand reached out to hers, taking it into a strong, warm grip. "I want to spend Christmas with you, Samantha. Not with her, or anyone else."

"I'm here," she said softly.

"Yes." His hand tightened around hers. "You're not just a temporary convenience, Samantha. Don't you know that?"

Her throat ached. "I'm not sure what I know, Ramsey."

For a moment her words hung in the silence.

"I'm not an easy man to know, I'm aware of that," he said then, his voice low. "It's become second nature to me to hide my feelings, not to let people get close to me."

His love and compassion had found other expressions. Samantha thought of the orphaned children for whom he made it possible to walk again and hear again, of Mrs. Gregory's sons, whom he was giving a future by paying for their education. She had a hunch there were other things.

She raised herself a little higher and leaned over, putting her face against his warm chest. She needed his closeness, the reassurance of his touch. His hand began to stroke her hair.

"When I'm with you, nothing else seems very important," he said huskily.

"I know," she whispered, feeling the solid beat of his heart against her cheek. She closed her eyes, savoring the sensation.

"Sometimes I call you just to hear your voice." He trailed his hand down the length of her hair and farther down, coming to rest in the small of her back. It lay there, warm and solid. The room was very quiet, with only the muted sound of their voices and the crackling of the fire breaking the stillness.

"I'm always thinking about you," she said. "I dream of you. You're never out of my mind."

Both his arms came around, lifting her higher up against him. "I need you, Samantha," he whispered against her hair. "I need you so."

With the soft-spoken words, the threads of desire weaved a web between them, a sense of magic that captured their senses.

She shifted her body restlessly against him. "Ramsey," she whispered, "let's make love."

Christmas morning. He was still sleeping when she awoke. It was still early, still dark outside. Samantha snuggled deeper under the covers and he stirred, mumbling something unintelligible, then reached out and drew her closer to him. Her face was pressed against the warmth of his neck. Closing her eyes, she smiled. There was nothing more delicious than this closeness and the slow stirring of desire.

Half asleep, Ramsey began to move his hands, stroking her, searching, caressing. She lay still for a while, absorbing his touch, savoring the pleasure, until the need to touch him too became too great. Turning on her side, she found his mouth, her hands searching his body. He gave a low groan, awake more fully now.

It was all warm and sweet sensation, a slow, languorous loving that stretched and lingered until tension mounted and she felt herself being swept away with him into a world of sunbursts.

They made breakfast together. She had insisted on doing it, rather than having it delivered. Even on Christmas morning such a thing was possible. For a price, of course.

She'd planned to make thick Belgian waffles from scratch, and she'd bought fresh strawberries imported from she knew not where, and a carton of whipping cream.

"I'll whip the cream," she said, as they busied themselves in the kitchen. "It's tricky. I like it nice and thick, but if you beat it too long you end up with butter. You make the waffles."

Ramsey poured batter on the waffle iron while she tended to the cream. The task done, she ejected the beaters. "Here, you lick one and I'll lick one. Unless," she said straightfaced, "you want them both."

He took the beater and looked at her. "I lick the beater?"

"Yes. You don't want to rinse all that lovely cream down the drain, do you? Haven't you ever licked the beater?"

"Not that I recall, no."

She shook her head. "A great deficiency in your upbringing."

"There were a few," he said dryly.

"Licking beaters was one of my favorite things when I was little." Samantha twirled her tongue sensuously around the beater, licking off the cream, her eyes challenging him. "Yum, delicious!"

Ramsey followed suit. She watched him, feeling mischief curl its little tentacles inside her. A headline like a neon light flickered in her mind. BILLIONAIRE LICKS MIXER BEATER.

"I know what you're thinking," he said, holding her gaze. "There's never an end to your little games, is there?"

She gave him an innocent look. "Games?"

"I can read your face like a book," he said, putting the tongue-gleaned beater in the sink. "Come here, you little witch."

He reached for her and she backed away, laughing. He moved toward her, took her face in his hands and kissed her, hard and deep. She pretended to struggle, but it was no use. She melted like ice cream sitting in the sun.

After he had kissed her more than thoroughly, he drew away a little, giving her a superior little smile. "Are you going to behave yourself?" he asked.

She met his eyes, trying not to laugh. "You wouldn't want me to."

After breakfast, there were the presents.

"I feel terrible," Samantha said, surveying the mounds of packages with her name on them.

"I'm going to enjoy watching you open them," said Ramsey, grinning. "Besides, I've got the best present of all, the one I really wanted."

She gave him a puzzled look.

"You," he said, smiling.

The expression on his face made her feel warm all over. "Thank you," she said, and kissed him. "I'm glad I'm here."

There were presents for Ramsey from Alicia's family, from his mother in Hawaii, from a few friends, and from Samantha.

He took the sweater out of its tissue-lined box, looked at it for an endless silent moment. "You *knitted* this?" he said then.

"Yes."

"It's beautiful. Not at all the handiwork of a little old lady."

"I'm not a little old lady. I use the latest European patterns." She laughed. "And then I adjust or modify them, of course."

"Of course," he agreed. "Otherwise all those creative energies would build up unused and who knows what might happen?"

"I'd turn neurotic, no doubt."

He pushed himself to his feet. "I'll go and put this on."

He came back a short while later. He looked magnificent. Samantha's heart leaped at the sight of him, wearing jeans, and the sweater over a blue shirt.

"It even looks better than I thought. I hope you like it."

He drew her close. "I do. And the fact that you made it for me with your own two hands makes it very special." He ran his fingers up through her hair, cupping her head in his hands. "You're a very special person, Samantha, you know that, don't you?"

"Why am I special?"

"You know how to give of yourself. You know how to love."

She felt her heart race. Did he know she loved him? Did he know without her having said it?

"You've enriched my life," he said quietly. "I know it sounds a little dramatic, but I don't know how else to say it. You've taught me to enjoy the small things in life." He smiled. "Like playing in the snow. Eating root soup. Licking whipped cream off a mixer beater."

Samantha felt her face flush. "You're embarrassing me, Ramsey."

He kissed her, a long, lingering kiss that left her breathless, a kiss that seemed to say a thousand words, expressed in the way he kissed her, the way he held her, the way he looked at her.

"You'd better open some more of your presents," he said, releasing her.

Her presents from family and friends consisted of books, gloves, music tapes, a nightgown, and a variety of items. From Ramsey she received a lovely kimono, and a framed charcoal drawing of a large African elephant. On the back it said, "For Samantha, who would like to set free elephants in zoos and men in dark suits. Ramsey."

It was a day she would never forget. They made Christmas dinner together, laughing, teasing. She felt light and delirious with love. Later they watched a French film on the VCR. They made love again.

Much of the rest of the week they spent together. They went out alone to places where it would be unlikely they'd meet people who knew them. They watched foreign movies, talked, made love. Ramsey spent only a minimum of time at his office. During the short periods he was gone, Samantha called Melissa and dealt with business related to ACTION, making sure everything was going well.

She tried not to think that in a matter of days she would be back in front of the class, that Ramsey would be in Japan on a business trip, that the period covered by the agreement was over. But fear slipped into her thoughts at odd moments, a fear that clenched her heart and made her hands tremble. She would stand in the middle of a room, or in front of a window, seeing nothing, feeling overwhelmed by panic.

Please, love me. Please, don't leave me.

She would force herself to calm down and the moment would pass.

For now she was happy. She loved him. She knew it with a certainty beyond any doubt, and it was a wonderful yet frightening knowledge.

"How about a ride in the country?" he asked the morning of New Year's Eve, their last full day together in his apartment. Tonight they would attend a lavish New

Year's Eve party, and some time tomorrow she would
go back to Aurora to be ready to teach again the next
day.

Please don't leave me.

She swallowed hard. "A ride in the country?"

"Yes. We did it once before, remember?"

"Oh, yes." She laughed. "It wasn't a great success,
but I'll go as long as you promise me we're not going
to talk business with one of your friends."

"It's a promise."

"Where are we going?"

"Leesburg."

She frowned. "Why?"

"It's a surprise." He dropped a kiss on her mouth.
"Believe me, you'll like it."

CHAPTER TWELVE

ALL the way to Leesburg Samantha tried, unsuccessfully, to trick the truth out of Ramsey. He simply was not to be tricked.

"It won't be a surprise if I tell you."

"True. How about a hint?"

"It's something I know you'll like." His eyes taunted her. "We're almost there."

The limousine moved through the center of town, slowing down as they reached the last few houses, then made a turn and moved up the driveway of the Foley house and stopped in front.

She looked at the house. It was finished now, or so it seemed. All painted, shutters replaced, the sagging front porch repaired, it was restored to new glory. A shiny brass knocker glimmered on the front door. "Why are we here?" she asked.

"You said you wanted to see the inside after it was finished."

"Yes, but..." Simon opened the door and reached out a hand to help her out of the car. Ramsey followed her out, ran quickly up the wooden steps and produced a key. He opened the door, turned and smiled at her.

"After you."

She stepped into the entryway. It was warm in the house and it smelled of wood and pine and floor wax. It was empty of furniture.

Ramsey closed the door and stepped in front of her. "Follow me, I'll give you the tour."

She glanced up at him. "How did you get the key?"

"I borrowed it from the owner."

"You went through all that trouble so I could see the inside of this house?"

170

"I wanted to see it myself. Let's start at the top and work our way down."

They climbed the wide, curving staircase with its smooth wooden handrail, polished to a high gloss. The bedrooms were large, with deep windows and oak floors. Everything had been painted and repaired. All the wood gleamed. There was a view of the gardens, which looked bare in their winter sleep.

"It will be beautiful when everything is green," Ramsey said. "In the spring the dogwoods and azaleas are magnificent, so I'm told."

She looked at him, something, a fragment of an idea, a thought, stirring in her mind. Then it was gone. They moved on, their footsteps sounding hollow in the empty rooms. Samantha tried to visualize what they'd look like with furniture in them. The bathrooms boasted all the comforts of modern technology, but were designed with the historic origins of the house in mind. Downstairs the kitchen as well had been fitted with all the modern appliances without having lost its historic charm.

"Wow, what a great kitchen!" Samantha exclaimed.

"You could really go to work in this one," he said.

She nodded, glancing at him again. Why was he showing her this house?

They moved through the dining room, the hall, the study, looking out of the windows.

"The heat works," he said. "It's nice and warm everywhere. They put in central air-conditioning too. Not bad."

Why was he telling her this? Why did he care? Why was he showing her this house? A vague suspicion began to form in her mind.

What if...?

No. She pushed the thought away, but it screamed for attention and her mind could not let go of it.

What if...?

No. She could not give in to her suspicion, the vague, delirious hope, because it was certainly too much to hope for, too much to expect.

What if the house was his? What if he had bought it and this was his way to... No, no. Samantha closed her eyes tightly and took in a deep breath. She could not allow herself to think the thought, not even in the silence and privacy of her own mind.

"And now the living room." Ramsey opened the heavy oak door and motioned her to enter ahead of him. She stepped inside, then stopped, her heart pounding so hard she was afraid it would jump right out of her chest. She could only stare.

A fire was crackling in the fireplace and in front of it on a large Oriental rug lay spread out a lavish culinary feast. Platters of food, bread, crystal glasses reflecting the flames, a bottle of champagne. Large cushions lay piled up for comfortable sitting.

Samantha licked her dry lips.

It's true, she thought wildly. He's changed his mind! He's going to ask me to marry him! We're going to live in this house!

"Are you hungry?" he asked.

She swallowed, trying to find her voice. "Yes." She swallowed again. "Oh, Ramsey, what a wonderful surprise!" She hugged him hard, feeling the solid bulk of his body against her own, feeling more happy than she'd felt in all her life.

He drew back a little and smiled at her. "You like the house?"

"Oh, Ramsey, you know I do! It's beautiful!"

His eyes smiled into hers.

"It's all yours," he said.

CHAPTER THIRTEEN

HAD she heard right? Was Ramsey giving the house to her? "Mine?" Samantha asked, her throat dry and painful.

"Yes. You can move in any time you like. You can live here and still teach and..."

She didn't hear what else he said. *You can live here. You can live here. You can live here.*

"Sit down," he said, taking her elbow. Gently he pushed her down on the large cushions, sitting down beside her.

She swallowed hard. "You bought this house for me?"

"Yes." He put his arm around her. "Did you think for a moment that I was going to let you go once the year was over?"

"I don't know."

She watched him as if in a trance as he opened the bottle of champagne, poured them each a glass, handing one to her. She could not feel her own body. She felt as if some terrible spell had been put on her. Despite the heat of the fire, she shivered.

You can live here. You can live here. You can live here.

"While I live in this house, where will you be?" she asked, and her voice seemed to come from very far away.

"I'll be in town. On the weekends, or whenever I get a chance, I'll be here with you. This will be our place, for just the two of us. I'll teach you how to ride a horse. We can have parties here. Or you can come into town and we can go to the ballet."

"Or to cocktail parties and business dinners." Her voice was toneless, but her tongue kept moving while her heart grew stone cold. She bit her lip and looked up at him. She could feel life flow back into her body again, feel her blood flood through her veins, feel the pain in her heart. "Did I ever tell you," she said slowly, praying for control, "about the people at those parties?"

Ramsey frowned. "What about them?"

She put the glass with champagne down on the hearth and put her hands in her lap. "They never take me at face value, you know." She sounded calm, in control. "They size me up, evaluate me, wonder who I am behind what they see, as if I'm hiding behind some disguise. They don't know where I come from or who I am." She paused and looked straight at him. "I know what they think, Ramsey," she went on softly, "and they don't think I'm a teacher. They laugh about that one, you know." She looked up at the ceiling and blinked furiously. "I could take it because I knew who I was and you knew who I was—at least, I thought so." She fought to keep her voice steady. "Now to you I've become exactly what they've been thinking I am all along." She swallowed, looking straight at him. "No, thank you." She came to her feet and made for the door. She had to leave. She couldn't bear to be here for another minute.

Ramsey jumped to his feet and pushed her back down on the cushions.

"I bought this house for you to make you happy," he told her.

She shrugged his hands off her shoulders and gave a cold, furious laugh. "You bought this house so you could have me! So you could put me in it and have me available whenever you wanted me!" She began to shake. "You make me feel like ... like a ..." Tears of rage blinded her eyes. "I *have* a house, Ramsey! I don't *need* a house! I don't need your money!"

There was a terrible silence. "My money was good enough a month ago," he said at last.

"That was a business contract! That was different, and you know it!"

"How was that different?"

"That money wasn't for me. I didn't sell you my body for money."

"You slept with me."

"Yes, I did." She felt a sinking sense of despair. "But that wasn't part of the agreement. I didn't do that for money, or to manipulate you, or to get anything out of you. I did it out of my own free will." She swallowed. "Because I wanted to." Because I *love* you.

Had he not understood that either? Did he not know the depth of her feelings for him?

"You can live in this house of your own free will."

She laughed, a bitter little laugh. "I'm not good enough for you, am I? I never was good enough. I'm only a schoolteacher. I don't belong in your exalted circles. Well, let me tell you something, Ramsey. I don't even want to belong. I like my own life a whole lot better than I like yours. I have real friends. I don't need your money. I don't need your house. And I don't need you!"

Head high, she marched out of the house, and this time he did not detain her. She walked into town, found a phone and called Melissa.

"Don't tell me you told me so," she said to Melissa. They were in Melissa's apartment, drinking herb tea, a special blend that was supposed to calm the nerves, or so the box said. Melissa had listened silently to Samantha's sorry tale.

"Is there anything I can do?" she asked.

"You can run me home. He's probably waiting for me there. I've still got to go to a New Year's Eve party with him tonight. One last gasp and that's it."

"You're still going? Are you nuts?" Melissa looked aghast.

"Of course I'm nuts. And of course I'm going. It's the very last of my assignments and then I can ask for the check and be done with him forever." Samantha gulped more tea. "I'm going to keep my end of the bargain. We can't risk losing the money for one lousy party. I'll live. All I have to do is look gorgeous and smile prettily. Don't worry, I'm an expert."

So Melissa drove her home. As expected, the limousine sat in the drive, ever patient. To her astonishment she saw Ramsey in the backyard, chopping wood in his grey pants and shirt, sleeves rolled up, blazer hanging from a tree branch.

She glanced at Melissa. "Look at that! Here's a sight you don't see often," she said.

Melissa laughed. "He's probably getting rid of his frustrations."

"Well, at least he's doing something useful." Samantha opened the car door. "Thanks. I'll call you when I get back tomorrow."

Melissa drove off and Samantha went up to Ramsey, who had stopped chopping wood and watched her approach.

"We can leave any time you're ready," she said calmly.

"Are you coming with me?"

"Yes," she said. "We have an agreement and I intend to keep it."

His jaw went rigid. "Damn the agreement!"

"I'd rather not, if you don't mind. We need the money," she said coolly, studying him. His hair was disheveled, his face grim, his hands balled into fists by his side. She'd never seen him look quite like that. He looked, somehow, out of control. It gave her a secret satisfaction. She turned and marched up to the limousine, and Simon hurried out to let her in.

Ramsey followed her. He opened the drinks cabinet. "Care for a drink?"

"No, thank you." She took a magazine from the rack and began to read, while Ramsey poured himself a Scotch.

"We have to talk," he said.

"No, we don't. I have absolutely nothing more to say to you."

"As you wish." He sat back and took a swallow of his drink, saying nothing more.

What a pair, she thought, as they sat in silence while the limousine moved down the road.

At the apartment, Mrs. Gregory was waiting for them with a light meal, after which Samantha escaped to her room and began to get ready for the ordeal of the night. She'd had time to compose herself. She was not going to fall apart. Not now, anyway. She was simply going to play her part, go through with the motions, and later, when she felt up to it, she would think. And then fall apart.

She slipped on the long silk cloqué dress, by far the most flamboyant thing she had bought with Ramsey's money. It was a dazzling multicolored affair, slightly gypsyish, with an off-the-shoulder neckline and a long, full, layered skirt. It was a playful, joyful dress, and she'd been delighted with the find, so perfect for a New Year's Eve party. Only now it seemed like a joke to put it on. The vibrant colors mocked her, making her feel like a fraud.

One more night, she said to herself. You can do it.

So she put on her happy face. She laughed. She smiled. She shook hands. She listened to people and talked when necessary, feeling dead inside. She was nothing more than a machine, working automatically when the right buttons were pushed. She had learned a lot in the last weeks. She could smile and pretend like the best of them.

She tried not to notice Ramsey's arm around her shoulders, the feel of his warm hand when he took hers. She didn't want him touching her, she didn't want to feel him so close while inside she felt this gaping distance separating them. But there was nothing to do about it; she simply had to suffer through it.

All through the evening she was aware of Ramsey's eyes on her. The dark, brooding expression on his face. He was not sure what to make of her behavior, but she didn't care. She had an agreement and she was going to keep it till the bitter end.

A large TV screen was erected at one end of the ballroom. They watched as the Times Square ball came down, inch by inch, ticking away the last seconds of the year. Then everybody was hugging and kissing and wishing everybody a Happy New Year to the tune of *Auld Lang Syne*. Ramsey drew her close against him, a kind of desperation in the firmness of his embrace. "Happy New Year," he said in her ear.

"Happy New Year," she returned. She had to say it, and of course she meant it. Then why was it so hard to say? His mouth closed over hers and, her whole body tense, she stood in his arms, fighting him, fighting herself.

He released her, stepping back, his eyes meeting hers. "Oh, God, Samantha," he said huskily, "don't fight me when I hold you."

Someone else grabbed her, kissed her and wished her a Happy New Year. Then another one and another one. She smiled, said Happy New Year, smiled some more until she was ready to scream.

But of course she did not.

She sat silently next to him as the limousine drove them back to his apartment, stood silently next to him as they went up in the elevator. Inside she wished him a good-night and went to her room.

She dropped down on the bed, feeling relief wash over her. This was it. No more parties.

She tossed and turned all night, giving up the fight for sleep at six. It was still dark outside and the house was silent; Ramsey must still be asleep. Slipping out of bed, she went into the kitchen to make coffee.

She might as well pack. Taking the coffee back to her room, she threw the few things she had brought with her into her suitcase, leaving all her party clothes in the closet. Maybe she could slip out before he awoke.

No such luck. As she was closing her suitcase, she noticed him standing in the door, wearing a blue robe. His hair was disheveled and his chin dark and unshaven.

"Isn't it a little early to leave?"

"I have things to do. I have to get ready for school."

Ramsey glanced at the open wardrobe. "The clothes are yours," he said.

"I don't want them." She lifted the suitcase off the bed. The clothes had never been hers. They were fairy-tale clothes, borrowed for a short time to create this wonderful illusion that now lay shattered at her feet. It was time to go back to the real world. *Adieu, la voiture, adieu, la boutique*. The ball was over and Cinderella had a hearth to sweep. Or at least a stove to clean out and start up again.

She glanced up at him, her mouth dry. "I have to go."

"Please don't go," he said, his voice husky. "Please stay with me. I need you."

She felt her heart contract, felt the pain deep inside, the temptation, briefly to just give in. To stay with him and love him on his own terms. Perhaps he would learn to love her the way she loved him.

No. She could not allow herself to fall into that trap.

"I have to go," she repeated.

"What do you want?"

"You know what I want." She looked right at him. "I want love. The real kind. The kind that comes with commitment and trust and loyalty." She took a deep breath. "But if you haven't got it, Ramsey, then there's no way to give it, is there? It's the one thing you can't go out and buy with money."

He closed his eyes, and for a fleeting moment pain rushed across his face. "I don't know anything about that kind of love."

She stared at him. "I'm sorry for you."

She turned, picked up her suitcase and walked out of the door.

A January bleaker and colder she could not remember. The days strung together in endless desolation.

It was her own fault. Melissa had been right all along: she should have used her head and not fallen in love with Ramsey. It had been a recipe for disaster from the very beginning. Not that the knowledge did her any good now.

She missed Ramsey—the way he smiled at her, the way he touched her. She fought against the pain, against the temptation to go back to him and love him on his own terms, accept his proposition. Maybe it was better than nothing. Maybe she could teach him to love her. Maybe she could show him how good it could be. Maybe...

But the image of the situation left her with a bad taste in her mouth. She wasn't for sale. Not at any price.

The official word had finally come. Aurora Elementary would be closed at the end of the school year. It was hard to believe, even though it had been expected.

"What are you going to do?" Melissa asked. "Apply for a job at the new schools?"

Samantha shrugged. "Paul and Lee Ann asked me to find a job in Philadelphia."

"Do you want to leave here?"

The thought of leaving Aurora and starting over somewhere else had insinuated itself into Samantha's mind over the last few weeks. Maybe this was her opportunity. Going to Philadelphia, however, did not appeal to her.

"Sometimes I think I do. I've been here all my life. Maybe I should see a little more of the world. Maybe we should both go, do something really outrageous and drastic."

Melissa laughed. "Outrageous sounds good. Let's join the Peace Corps together. Go to some place where it's warm and nobody has ever seen snow. Or, alternatively, we can go to Alaska."

"It's *cold* in Alaska."

"There are men there, Samantha. Many, many men, and almost no single women."

"I'm not going to look at another man for the rest of my life."

"Of course, I forgot about that." Melissa sighed theatrically. "Well then, we can bury ourselves in the sands of Chad, or the jungles of Bolivia. They can use teachers and nurses anywhere. The world is ours."

Samantha studied Melissa's face. "Would you really want to leave and do something like that?" she asked.

"For a couple of years? Why not? If we don't like it, we can always come back."

Samantha's birthday was at the end of the month, and, against all her wishes, Melissa had organized a party for her. "It'll do you good," she said.

"I don't want a party, Melissa. All I want is to wallow in my misery."

"Well, we won't let you."

"I have the right to wallow in my own misery!"

"Don't be difficult, Sam. We'll have a good time. Everybody will be there."

She could not refuse to go. Well, she knew how to put on a happy face.

So she did. And she had to admit it did cheer her up. Being with friends, laughing, telling jokes, it all helped. For a while.

It was late when finally she got into her car, her arms full of presents. The night was cold, with a clouded sky, a full moon and few visible stars.

She parked the car and went around the back. She looked up at the sky, at the cold moon. She sat down on a large, uncut log and huddled in her jacket. Who said the moon was romantic? It seemed cold and sinister peeping through the clouds with the stark black branches of the naked trees swaying in front of it.

Despite the warmth and friendship of the evening, she felt bitterly alone. A dark, gaping loneliness that ached inside her. Her house seemed empty. Her life seemed empty.

She was a strong person. Everybody thought she was, but she didn't feel strong. She felt as if inside her she was withering away with grief, and one day, not long from now, there wouldn't be anything left of her heart. How could this have happened to her? How could she be so hopelessly in love with a man who was clearly wrong for her? They were questions of the rational mind. Her heart didn't care about the questions or the answers. Her heart only felt the pain and the longing.

Her eyes misted over. "Oh, Ramsey," she whispered, "what am I going to do? How can I forget you?"

She got up slowly, feeling suddenly how cold she was. Shivering, she moved toward the house, her legs stiff and wooden. It didn't help to feel sorry for herself. There was so much to be grateful for—good friends, a profession she loved, her own house. Why couldn't she be happy with her blessings?

Before she had met Ramsey she had been. Before she had met Ramsey she hadn't really known how much she wanted someone for herself, one person to whom she would be the most important woman in the world. One person to share her life with, the good and the bad, one person to love and cherish.

Ramsey had been willing to give her everything— everything except the one thing she wanted most, the one thing that would have to come from his heart, not his wallet.

And what he wanted from her he wanted for money, so that there would be no other obligation. Only he didn't understand that what she offered him freely could never be given in exchange for money or possessions. It held value only when given freely and unconditionally.

She took out her key and inserted it into the back door. It wasn't locked. She frowned. David had come to collect the bags of food she had put together before she had gone to the party. He must have forgotten to lock the door. She sighed and closed the door behind her, then took off her jacket and hung it up.

One day there would be another man, a man she could love. They'd get married, have children. Only she couldn't visualize herself with anyone. All she saw in her mind was Ramsey.

Maybe if she just moved quickly, got into bed and went to sleep, she wouldn't notice how empty the house was. Carrying the two plastic bags with her gifts, she moved into the living room.

Her heart stood still. The house wasn't empty.

Ramsey, wearing the sweater she'd knitted for him, was sitting by the fire.

CHAPTER FOURTEEN

"RAMSEY?" Samantha whispered. "Is that you?" For a terrifying moment she wondered if she were hallucinating, if dreaming of him coming back to her had actually made her mind believe it was so. No lights were on. Only the red glow of the fire illuminated his dark shape in the chair.

"I didn't mean to frighten you," he said.

"No." She swallowed hard. "I... I just didn't expect you here."

"It's your birthday," he said, as if that explained everything.

She switched on a light. He was still there. "My friends..." She swallowed again. She was shaking and she could hardly get the words out. "My friends had a party for me." She dropped the plastic bags on the couch.

"Are those your presents?" he asked.

She nodded. She ran her tongue over her cold, dry lips. "I thought you were in Japan."

"I cut my trip short."

"Oh." She hugged herself, still shivering. "Where's Simon? I didn't see the limo."

"I told him to find a hotel. I had no idea how long I had to wait for you."

"I see." She moved in front of the stove and held out her hands to warm them. He had opened the doors and put in the screen and a big fire roared inside. The heat comforted her.

"You're freezing," he said. "Why were you out so long?"

"Was I?"

"I heard your car. I wondered why you didn't come in right away."

"I was looking at the moon. It looked eerie." There was something terribly unreal about what was going on, about Ramsey being here, about the polite words spoken in the silent room.

"Can I get you something warm? Some cocoa?"

She nodded, and he came to his feet and moved into the kitchen.

She looked at his empty chair. He was gone. He hadn't really been here at all—of course he hadn't. She was going crazy, imagining things. He wasn't in the kitchen making her hot chocolate. She was dreaming. Soon she would wake up and she would know it had all been a dream. She couldn't stop shivering. Sitting down in a chair by the fire, she closed her eyes and tried to concentrate on the warmth of the fire, feeling it radiate on to her legs and arms and face.

"Here you go." Ramsey held out a steaming mug of hot chocolate. She took it from him.

"Thank you." She looked up at his face. "Why are you here?"

He sat down in the chair opposite her. He closed his eyes briefly, as if to gather himself. Then his eyes met hers, his face tense. "I need you," he said huskily.

Her hands shook so much, she put the cup down on the hearth. She clenched her hands together, looking at him, not speaking.

"These last few weeks," he said slowly, the words coming with difficulty, "without you my life is so...cold. There's no joy, no color, no warmth."

She felt hot tears behind her eyes. She bit her lip, staring into the fire.

"Samantha, I want your warmth, your laughter, your love." Ramsey paused, struggling with himself. "And I was wrong, so terribly wrong, to think that it was for sale. When you came into my life, I was offered the most precious gift of all, and I didn't know. I didn't recognize it and I threw it away."

"Ramsey..."

He held up his hand. "Please, just let me say this. I need to say this. I want you, Samantha, but I know that the only way I'm going to have you is if you're willing to give yourself to me of your own free will." He rubbed his neck. "You said that I think you're not good enough for me. Well, you're wrong. You're too good for me."

"That's not true."

"Oh, yes, it is. I'm a selfish bastard, Samantha. You're quite right that I think I can have everything I want because I have money and power. Well, you taught me a lesson."

She sipped the cocoa, not knowing what to say.

"I wanted you from the moment I saw you in that run-down little school of yours," he went on. "You were so different from anyone I'd ever met. You were so un-selfconscious, so without pretense, I couldn't help but be intrigued. You weren't at all impressed by me, were you? You thought of it all as a big joke."

"So you made up that scheme of needing me to keep the vultures away."

He gave a crooked smile. "No, not really. It was true enough, but I could have found someone else. I just didn't want someone else. I wanted you."

"You kept me at a distance for a long time."

"You were falling in love with me. And, believe it or not, I was uncomfortable with my own feelings. Besides, you had me sign that damned piece of paper."

She stared into the flames. Her feelings were chaotic. She couldn't think of anything to say.

"I love you, Samantha," he said softly. "I think I loved you from the day I met you, from the moment you shoved that box in my hands and told me to go stand in line."

She looked up at him and tears came to her eyes. "You never told me you loved me."

"I was afraid."

She looked at his face, that strong, controlled face. "Afraid of what?" she asked softly.

"Of being vulnerable. Of losing. But I know I have to take that risk. I have no choice. I love you so, Samantha."

"I love you too," she whispered.

Coming to his feet, he stood in front of her. He took something out of his pocket and pressed it into her hands. "Happy birthday," he said.

It was a small velvet box, unwrapped. Her heart pounded so loud, it was frightening. She flipped open the lid. On a bed of dark satin lay a ring—a plain, wide gold band. No diamonds, no precious stones.

As a symbol it was invaluable.

Tears ran over; she could no longer hold them back. She began to cry, and suddenly she was enveloped in his embrace, her face against his chest.

"Marry me," he said. "Please marry me. I love you, I don't want to be without you."

"Oh, Ramsey," she whispered, "you don't believe in marriage."

He kissed the tears from her cheeks. "The alternative is terrifying. I can't live without you, Samantha. I want you with me for the rest of my life. I'll do whatever it takes to make you happy. You can come with me on my trips and see the world, or you can teach if you want to, or you can start your own charity program with the MacMillan Corporation and help whomever you want to, just as long as you never leave me."

She laughed through her tears. "Oh, Ramsey, is there a condition for everything?"

"You didn't answer my question. Will you please marry me?"

"Yes," she said, feeling joy rush through her like champagne. "Yes, I'll marry you, Ramsey MacMillan."

POSTCARDS FROM EUROPE

HARLEQUIN PRESENTS®

Hi—

Have arrived safely in Germany, but Diether von Lössingen denies that he's the baby's father. Am determined that he shoulder his responsibilities!

Love, Sophie

P.S. Diether's shoulders are certainly wide enough.

Take 4 bestselling love stories FREE

Plus get a FREE surprise gift!

Special Limited-time Offer

Mail to Harlequin Reader Service®

3010 Walden Avenue
P.O. Box 1867
Buffalo, N.Y. 14269-1867

YES! Please send me 4 free Harlequin Presents® novels and my free surprise gift. Then send me 6 brand-new novels every month, which I will receive months before they appear in bookstores. Bill me at the low price of $2.44 each plus 25¢ delivery and applicable sales tax, if any*. That's the complete price and—compared to the cover prices of $2.99 each—quite a bargain! I understand that accepting the books and gift places me under no obligation ever to buy any books. I can always return a shipment and cancel at any time. Even if I never buy another book from Harlequin, the 4 free books and the surprise gift are mine to keep forever.

106 BPA ANRH

Name	(PLEASE PRINT)	
Address	Apt. No.	
City	State	Zip

This offer is limited to one order per household and not valid to present Harlequin Presents® subscribers. *Terms and prices are subject to change without notice. Sales tax applicable in N.Y.

UPRES-94R   ©1990 Harlequin Enterprises Limited

My Valentine 1994

Celebrate the most romantic day of the year with
MY VALENTINE 1994
a collection of original stories, written by
four of Harlequin's most popular authors...

MARGOT DALTON
MURIEL JENSEN
MARISA CARROLL
KAREN YOUNG

Available in February, wherever
Harlequin Books are sold.

HARLEQUIN ®

VAL94

HARLEQUIN®

Don't miss these Harlequin favorites by some of our most distinguished authors!
And now, you can receive a discount by ordering two or more titles!

HT#25409	THE NIGHT IN SHINING ARMOR by JoAnn Ross	$2.99	☐
HT#25471	LOVESTORM by JoAnn Ross	$2.99	☐
HP#11463	THE WEDDING by Emma Darcy	$2.89	☐
HP#11592	THE LAST GRAND PASSION by Emma Darcy	$2.99	☐
HR#03188	DOUBLY DELICIOUS by Emma Goldrick	$2.89	☐
HR#03248	SAFE IN MY HEART by Leigh Michaels	$2.89	☐
HS#70464	CHILDREN OF THE HEART by Sally Garrett	$3.25	☐
HS#70524	STRING OF MIRACLES by Sally Garrett	$3.39	☐
HS#70500	THE SILENCE OF MIDNIGHT by Karen Young	$3.39	☐
HI#22178	SCHOOL FOR SPIES by Vickie York	$2.79	☐
HI#22212	DANGEROUS VINTAGE by Laura Pender	$2.89	☐
HI#22219	TORCH JOB by Patricia Rosemoor	$2.89	☐
HAR#16459	MACKENZIE'S BABY by Anne McAllister	$3.39	☐
HAR#16466	A COWBOY FOR CHRISTMAS by Anne McAllister	$3.39	☐
HAR#16462	THE PIRATE AND HIS LADY by Margaret St. George	$3.39	☐
HAR#16477	THE LAST REAL MAN by Rebecca Flanders	$3.39	☐
HH#28704	A CORNER OF HEAVEN by Theresa Michaels	$3.99	☐
HH#28707	LIGHT ON THE MOUNTAIN by Maura Seger	$3.99	☐

Harlequin Promotional Titles

#83247	YESTERDAY COMES TOMORROW by Rebecca Flanders	$4.99	☐
#83257	MY VALENTINE 1993	$4.99	☐
	(short-story collection featuring Anne Stuart, Judith Arnold, Anne McAllister, Linda Randall Wisdom)		

(limited quantities available on certain titles)

	AMOUNT	$
DEDUCT:	10% DISCOUNT FOR 2+ BOOKS	$
ADD:	POSTAGE & HANDLING	$
	($1.00 for one book, 50¢ for each additional)	
	APPLICABLE TAXES*	$ _____
	TOTAL PAYABLE	$ _____
	(check or money order—please do not send cash)	

To order, complete this form and send it, along with a check or money order for the total above, payable to Harlequin Books, to: **In the U.S.:** 3010 Walden Avenue, P.O. Box 9047, Buffalo, NY 14269-9047; **In Canada:** P.O. Box 613, Fort Erie, Ontario, L2A 5X3.

Name: _____

Address: _____ City: _____

State/Prov.: _____ Zip/Postal Code: _____

*New York residents remit applicable sales taxes.
 Canadian residents remit applicable GST and provincial taxes.

HBACK-JM